the seven magpies

Also by Monica Hughes

the seven magpies

MONICA HUGHES

HarperPaperbacks
A Division of HarperCollinsPublishers

http://www.harpercollins.com/canada

First published in hardcover by HarperCollins Publishers Ltd: 1996
First HarperCollins Publishers Ltd mass market edition: 1997

Canadian Cataloguing in Publication Data

Hughes, Monica, 1925–
   The seven magpies

ISBN 0-00-224549-3 (bound) ISBN 0-00-648109-4 (pbk)

I. Title.

PS8565.U34S48 1996   jC813'.54   C96-930741-1
PZ7.H87364Se 1996

---

97 98 99 ❖ OPM 10 9 8 7 6 5 4 3 2 1

Printed and bound in the United States

To my war-time friends

CHAPTER ONE

"It's an excellent school and you'll soon make lots of friends." It was a peace offering, wrapped and tied with a ribbon. Maureen Frazer ignored it. "You'll get to like it, I know you will," her mother went on firmly.

You'll get to like it. *Parents have been saying that to their children forever*, Maureen thought. *Eve probably said it to Cain and Abel after they were chucked out of the Garden of Eden, and look what happened then.* She stared grimly out of the window as the train suddenly jerked and began to move slowly out of Saint Andrews station.

Staring at the glass she could see the houses sliding slowly by, the washing on the lines, everything ordinary and everyday; or she could blink and see the reflection of her own face. She played at changing focus quickly, so that her bushy mop of carroty hair and pale freckly face overlaid the fields and trees. It was as if she were being spread as thin as butter on toast across the breadth of Scotland, leaving a little bit of herself behind all the way. *If I'm not careful,* she thought, *I'll be invisible by the time I reach Oban.*

Behind her reflection something moved, and she turned to see that Mother was already buttoning her tweed jacket, adjusting her brown felt hat. The first part of the journey was already almost over, just the half hour between Saint Andrews and Dundee. Mother stood up and lifted down the two cases from the webbing rack above the murky photographs of Loch Lomond and Princes Street.

"I can't possibly wear my old uniform to the new school," Maureen had protested as she'd watched Mother pack those same cases the day before. "I'll be different."

"There's a war on. They'll understand."

But Maureen knew they wouldn't. As the train slowed she looked down at her navy blazer, edged with purple and white braid, and the pleated tunic under it. At Logan Academy for Young Ladies, she knew, the blazers were dark green with a gold crest on the breast pocket, and the girls wore skirts instead of tunics. I'll stick out like a lump of coal, she thought miserably.

"Don't dawdle, dear." Mother prodded her in the back with the cases, and she had to jump down to the platform. "Three hours until your train leaves, and goodness knows whether you'll get anything to eat on it, the muddle things are in. We'll put the cases in the Left Luggage, do a little shopping and then have a bite."

"I'm not hungry," Maureen said automatically.

Mother gave a small, patient sigh. "Do try to be a little more cooperative, dear. You know it's for your own good. The east coast of Scotland is a possible invasion area. You'll be much safer at boarding school."

"None of my friends is going. Not a single one. Their parents think Saint Andrews is safe enough. I don't see why . . ."

Another sigh, not so patient. "We've been through all this before. With your father away . . ."

Maureen's father was in the reserves and had been called into active service even before the third of September. Maureen shivered, remembering that sunny Sunday, over a week ago, when Britain had declared war on Germany after the Nazis had invaded Poland. The awful wail of the siren had come right after the BBC broadcast on the wireless. She remembered how they had stared out across the North Sea, wondering what they would see. Enemy ships? Or airplanes filling the sky? It had been the scariest moment in Maureen's life, until the "all clear" had sounded.

But, scary or not, at least we were together, she thought now. *Daddy, Mother and me. Together.*

Then Daddy left, handsome in his officer's uniform, and Mother had already volunteered for the WRNS.

Because of all the work she'd done on hospital and symphony boards and things like that, she was going to be an officer in a smart uniform organizing things and bossing new recruits about.

"But what about me?" Maureen had wailed. "I'll be all alone." And that's when Mother had broken it to her that she was to go to Logan Academy, which had decided to evacuate its boarders to a safe area.

"You mean I'll be stuck in the west of Scotland and miss all the fun? It isn't fair!"

"War isn't fun, Maureen. Don't be so childish," Mother had snapped. But even though she'd frowned and tightened her lips, Maureen knew, from the way her mother's eyes shone and the speed with which she organized everything, that she couldn't wait to leave Saint Andrews and boss Wrens about in a big city like Edinburgh or London.

So here she was, Maureen Frazer, fourteen years old, abandoned by father and mother, practically an orphan, about to spend the duration of the war in some old castle in the west of Scotland, miles and miles from her friends and from films and dancing class and everything else that made life worth living.

The Duration. It was a word on everybody's lips these days, a word with a brand new meaning. Only, how long was the Duration going to be? She trailed after her mother to the Left Luggage office and then out of the station. At any other time a day trip to Dundee was something to look forward to. But not today. And Mother's idea of a little shopping was to stock up on boring vests and knickers and beige cotton stockings.

"Can't I at least have a lipstick?"

"*Try* not to be annoying, Maureen. You know perfectly well that fourteen is far too young for make-up. Wait till you leave school."

They had tea and scones at the station hotel, the tea so strong that Maureen could feel it coating her teeth; but its warmth was comforting and, though she wasn't really hungry, the scones helped fill up the miserable hollow in her middle.

The luggage was reclaimed and Mother piled the cases and the parcels into a compartment on the Oban train.

"I'll never manage all that at the other end, Mother. Can't you post the parcels to me?"

"You can't trust the post these days. I'm sure you'll be able to tuck them all into your cases if you try, dear. Oh, there's the whistle! Got your ticket? Your gas mask? Your money? Goodbye." Mother hugged her suddenly and unexpectedly, and Maureen found herself clinging to her, the tweed jacket rough against her cheek, the familiar scent of Coty face powder and eau de cologne in her nose.

"When will I ever see you again! Oh, Mother, please don't make me—"

But Mother had jumped from the carriage. The door was slammed and the train jerked forward. Maureen pulled down the window above the door and leaned out, reaching for Mother's gloved hand.

The train moved faster so she had to let go and wave frantically at the slim figure dwindling away into the distance.

"And we'll have that window shut, if you please. The smuts are a' coming in."

Reluctantly Maureen drew her head in and tugged on the strap that pulled the window up. There were three other people in the compartment, one for each corner seat. The woman who had just spoken was dressed in black, her grey hair in a bun as tight as a stone. The other two corners were occupied by farmers in well-worn tweeds and boots, their faces ruddy and weather-beaten.

She blinked hard. She couldn't possibly let these curious strangers see how close she was to tears. She busied herself by opening her cases and trying to fit into them the underwear that Mother had just bought. She felt stupid as she undid the parcels and flattened the vests and knickers on top of her other clothes, and she hoped the two men would pay no attention to what she was doing.

"That looks like good quality stuff," the old woman remarked. "But awfu' light. In my day we had combinations; fleece-lined they were."

"Aye," one of the farmers responded. "There's nothing like good fleece next to the skin."

Her face flaming, Maureen pushed the last pairs of cotton stockings into the cases, leaned on the lids and snapped the locks shut.

"I'll just be putting those up on the rack for you

then," one of the farmers offered. "Would you be travelling far, young lady?"

"To Oban."

"Oban. Och, aye."

"You'll be having to change at Dunblane then," the other farmer volunteered.

Maureen stared at him in dismay. Then she took the pasteboard ticket from her purse. It said nothing about changing anywhere. Did the man know what he was talking about? Suppose she got off the train at Dunblane and it went on, leaving her stranded? Suppose she stayed on and it did go somewhere else and not to Oban? Why hadn't Mother said? Why had Mother left her alone? She swallowed and blinked hard.

The woman in black reached across and patted her knee. "You can be asking the conductor when he comes through to clip the tickets."

Maureen nodded and felt a little braver. "Thank you," she whispered.

The train rocked gently to and fro, and the rhythmic clatter of the wheels over the rails lulled her into a doze. She and Mother had been up late the night before, packing Maureen's school clothes and arguing over whether she could possibly fit any of her favourite books into her two cases.

"Honestly, you're so like your father!" Mother had exclaimed. "Your nose always in a book. A dose of reality will do you no harm at all." Mother had won in the end. She almost always did. The best that Maureen could do was to slip her copy of *Kidnapped* into her blazer pocket to read on the train.

"Do you think Daddy will have books over in France?" she'd asked, and Mother's face had suddenly got a pinched look, as if she were cold—or scared.

But all she'd said was, "I'm sure he'll be *far* too busy for reading. Now off to bed with you."

A goodnight kiss. A pat on the shoulder. Then Maureen had gone to bed and to a night of dreams, dreams full of anxious packings and waiting for trains that never came, finding herself standing on empty platforms dressed only in her underwear.

"Will you have a sweetie, my dear?"

She opened her eyes and blinked. The old woman was holding out a paper bag.

"Thank you." The humbug was dark brown and powerfully pepperminty. The old woman offered the bag to the two farmers.

"I'll not say no to a good sweetie."

"We'll not be seeing them for a while," the other added.

"Aye, there'll be rationing and all. Like last time." The old woman nodded. "They'll be cutting sugar, that's certain."

They sat sucking in peaceful silence, while the landscape flashed by, hills on the one side and the Firth of Tay on the other. Then the train slowed down and they were in Perth.

After Perth the conductor came down the corridor, clipping their tickets and confirming what the farmer had said, that she'd have to leave the train at Dunblane and get on the train that came through from Edinburgh to Oban. "It'll be a wee wait. You'll have plenty of time to get a sandwich, for you won't be in Oban before four and you'll be clemmed by then."

"Och, I wouldna count on a station buffet in a wee place like Dunblane," the old woman interrupted.

Before the conductor could get into an argument with her about the quality of food on Scottish railways, Maureen said quickly, "Thank you. My mother bought me a sandwich in Dundee."

"Aye, that'll be best then." The old woman nodded. Afterwards, in the thirty-odd miles before they got to Dunblane, she bombarded Maureen with questions, and the whole story of Daddy being in the army and Mother volunteering for the Wrens came out. "And the school's in a kind of castle in the Highlands, somewhere south of Oban."

"That's no strictly the Highlands," one of the farmers put in.

"This place is on Loch Kintray."

"Och, that's only twenty miles or so south of Loch Linnhe," said the other farmer.

"Nevertheless, that's twenty miles south o' the Highlands." And they went on arguing until the old lady passed round the humbugs again.

By the time the train reached Dunblane and they handed down her luggage and waved goodbye, Maureen felt they were old friends. The train pulled out, leaving her alone on the deserted platform.

The train from Edinburgh was full, and instead of having a window seat she was squashed between two fat women. Nobody offered to help her put her cases on the rack. In fact, the rack was already piled high, and she had to tuck her cases under the seat, where their sharp edges dug into her calves for the rest of the journey.

Nobody talked to anybody, and nobody handed round peppermints. Maureen unwrapped her sandwich from its grease-proof paper wrapper. It was ham, dried out at the edges, with just a smear of yellow mustard to make it interesting. When she'd finally got the last bite down she had to walk along the swaying corridor to the lavatory to get a drink of water.

After her lunch she took her book out of her pocket and began to read, her toes curling with pleasure at the familiar words and the exciting adventure that lay ahead:

> I will begin the story of my adventures
> with a certain morning early in the month
> of June, the year of grace 1751, when I
> took the key for the last time out of the
> door of my father's house . . .

Maureen paused and looked out of the train window. The countryside was strange to her, hilly, the slopes pinky mauve with heather. The places they stopped at were villages, just a few grey-stone houses and a kirk.

She was starting out on an adventure of her own this day, "early in the month of September, the year of grace 1939." Would anything as exciting happen to her as happened to David Balfour in the Highlands of Scotland in 1751? She read on.

"Loch Awe." A woman by the window broke the long silence, and Maureen craned her neck to see a lake so long that the end of it was lost in mist. "Just a wee while to Oban."

"That's careless talk. Naming names. There could be a spy among us the now."

The woman flushed. "Och, that's foolish. As if a body didna ken Loch Awe!"

Spies, thought Maureen, with a shiver of excitement. Like in one of John Buchan's adventure stories. It was possible, wasn't it? All sorts of things were possible now there was a war on. Spies could parachute into the countryside, disguised as nuns, she had heard, though that sounded foolish, since a nun would show up a mile off. Or they could sneak ashore from boats or submarines. Ireland was just across the water, and Ireland was neutral—but friendlier to Germany than Britain, some said.

She looked cautiously at the people jammed into the carriage. They all looked very ordinary, very Scottish. She hadn't told them that *she* hadn't known the great lake they'd passed was Loch Awe. They might think that *she* was a spy.

When the train finally pulled into Oban she hauled her cases from under the seat, slung her gas-mask case over her shoulder and jumped thankfully down to the platform. Mother had given her directions. What were they? "Ask the ticket collector to tell you where to catch the Lochgilphead bus. It goes past the lodge gate, and they'll have arranged for a taxi to meet you and take you up to the house." A taxi? From gate to house? Why couldn't she walk?

It was a sunny day, with the sun dancing brilliantly on the blue water, the breeze barely filling the sails of the small fishing boats out in the bay. She sat on the bench at the bus stop, getting hotter and thirstier by the minute, afraid to move away in case the bus came early.

It arrived at last and bumped south along a road that twisted and turned, dodging the sea that pushed fingers of water into the rocky shore. It was an interesting, though untidy, landscape. She remembered a story about God making the world and how, when He'd finished, He'd tossed the last scraps of land out of His apron into the sea, where they became the Western Highlands and Islands.

"You're for the lodge, then, Missy?" The driver's voice interrupted her thoughts. He pulled the bus to the side of the narrow road, and she got out and stood by while he hauled out her cases for her. "You're waited for, then?"

"What? Oh, yes, there's supposed to be a taxi. I don't see one. I could walk up to the lodge, couldn't I?"

"With your luggage? I wouldna suggest it. Bide there. Dinna fret. I'm a minute or so early. Your taxi will be on its way."

Kintray Lodge, the sign said in peeling paint on a battered board. An unpaved road led through rough meadowland along the edge of a sea loch and vanished around a headland. Highland cattle, with hides like hearthrugs and great horns curving like bicycle handles, grazed in the meadow. One of them raised its shaggy head to look at her. She decided she'd better wait for the taxi after all and sat down on her cases. It was very hot and, apart from the cattle, there was not a living thing in sight. *Suppose no one comes. What'll I do then?*

At last a plume of dust appeared in the south and turned into the taxicab. Maureen swallowed her panic and got to her feet.

"You'll be Miss Frazer?" the driver asked cautiously, as if there were queues of people waiting for taxis. "Hop in then."

He didn't offer to help with her cases, and she hauled them onto the back seat and got in beside them. The seat was made of stuff that prickled the backs of her legs, and the taxi smelt of pipe tobacco, old socks and fish, but it was her rescuer and by now she didn't care.

They bumped along the road, past the fierce-looking cattle, up the hill and through a thicket of what Maureen realized must be rhododendrons. Now, in September, they were dark and gloomy, though in the spring they must be beautiful. *But I won't be here*, she promised herself fiercely. *By spring the war will be over. Everyone says so.*

Suddenly the taxicab emerged into sunshine and onto a kind of plateau. She glimpsed lawns, a gravel driveway and the lodge itself. Grey granite. Two storeys here; four there. Turrets, and gables shaped like steps. A castle, magical and mysterious, was her first thought. Her second was, What a wonderful place for hide-and-seek! The taxi followed the sweep of the driveway round to the front of the house and stopped by an enormous doorway, above which was a crest carved in stone.

Maureen paid the man, anxiously calculating the tip, picked up her cases and crunched across the gravel. As the door was ajar she pushed it cautiously open and walked into the shadows of a vast hall. The floor was tiled, and the panelled walls rose up two storeys. Over doors and windows stared the shaggy horned heads of enormous stags. Above them, moving slightly in the breeze from the open door, hung faded banners and flags. Directly opposite her a grandfather clock ticked solemnly, and a barometer showed "set fair." A long way off there were girls' voices and a sudden peal of laughter.

Like an ocean wave, homesickness washed over Maureen and battered at her defences. The weight on her chest was so heavy she couldn't breathe. She could feel a sob rising inside her like a hiccough, a sob that threatened to explode into a noisy outburst. She told herself sternly to be strong, the way Daddy had been strong when he left for France. She dug her handkerchief—regulation white cotton, sixteen inches square—out of her blazer pocket and blew her nose loudly.

A door to her left opened and a woman came out. She was extremely tall and lean, rather like a pipecleaner figure dressed in a tweed skirt, white blouse and pearl necklace. Her face was ruddy and leathery, like the sailor's in the advertisements on buses for lifeboat appeals. In her longing for comfort, all Maureen could think was, *She has no bosom*. Which was stupid. Mother had no bosom either, or at least not the kind one could throw oneself against for a comforting hug.

"My dear child, I do apologize. I intended to be waiting at the door to welcome you, but I got diverted. There is still so much organization to be done. As you know, we moved in only ten days ago. I am Miss Priestley, the headmistress. Welcome to Logan Academy."

Maureen shook the proffered hand. It was firm and dry, the handshake decisive.

"You must be exhausted. What a marathon journey! Leave your luggage in the hall for the moment and come into my study."

It was a pretty room, the pattern of the flowered wallpaper echoed in the curtains in the bay window and on the cretonne covers of the chairs. An imposing mahogany desk filled the left corner of the room, but in the centre two easy chairs and a small sofa had been drawn up to a low round table, on which sat a large teapot, flanked by plates of Dundee cake and shortbread.

Two cups of tea later she began to feel better. Miss Priestley's conversation about the history of Logan Academy washed over her, an incomprehensible background to the reality of tea and food. She realized guiltily that she should be paying attention. She put down her cup and tried to look intelligent.

"We accept students aged twelve and up," Miss Priestley was saying. "We have always prided ourselves on maintaining small classes and high academic standards. Though we may have to 'make do' in some respects for the duration, our standards will not slip. Not only do we expect to see our students taking their place in society as intelligent, well-bred young ladies, but we also expect to see them making their mark in the professions—teaching, of course, but also in social work, possibly even medicine. Have you considered *your* future, Maureen?"

"N-no, Miss Priestley." *I'm not going to be here long enough for you to worry about my future*, she wanted to say, but of course couldn't.

The headmistress smiled. "You'll be taking your Junior Oxford Certificate this year. You still have plenty of time to decide. Now, if you are sufficiently refreshed, I will show you the room you will be sharing with your Lower Fifth friends. You will have an hour to unpack and wash and change before dinner, which is at six precisely. You will hear the gong."

Change. Into what? "I don't have an academy uniform, Miss Priestley," Maureen stammered. "Just my tunic."

"Oh, dear, yes. Of course. Perhaps a fresh blouse? Who knows for how long this war may go on, or how many sacrifices we may have to make? Clothes rationing, I predict, before we're through, as well as food rationing. Now, follow me. Can you manage your cases?"

Maureen meekly followed the straight, lean back up the wide polished stairs and then up a narrower flight. "Your form has its dormitory on the third floor, with the Upper Fifth. The bathroom is here." A door was opened briefly to show a row of basins. "Baths are limited, I'm afraid, to one a week. There is a list as to your particular time. The water for the house comes from a spring up on the hill, and we have been warned to be careful. But I do expect my young ladies to take a daily sponge bath. No slacking! The lavatories are next door. And here is your dormitory."

Dormitory. The word brought back memories of schoolgirl adventure stories, of midnight feasts and larks. Maybe boarding school was going to be all right after all. It might even be fun. Everything depended on her form mates.

Miss Priestley pushed open the door and Maureen found herself in what must once have been an elegant bedroom, in the days when the lodge was filled with sportsmen and their wives enjoying weekends of hunting, fishing and partying. Now the canopied bed, which would have occupied the centre of the room back then, had been pushed against one wall and six small cots had been crammed in beside it. Two wardrobes and three chests of drawers, none of them matching, filled the remaining space. There was barely room to walk between the beds or to open the drawers.

Miss Priestley gave a short bark of laughter at the expression on Maureen's face. "It does require a certain degree of tact and mutual accommodation for eight young ladies to dress or disrobe in the limited space. But the girls seem to be managing well enough, and I'm sure you'll fit in beautifully."

"You say there will be eight of us, Miss Priestley? But there are only seven beds here."

"I know. A slight logistical problem. Impossible, as you see, to cram in an extra bed, however narrow. The alternative was to put you in the Lower Fourth dormitory, which is a larger room, but that hardly seemed fair to you. However, that four-poster could sleep a battalion. With a bolster down the middle, I am sure two of the girls will be most comfortable in it, and all will work out satisfactorily."

Briskly Miss Priestley opened and shut drawers and showed Maureen where she could hang her clothes. "And here is a towel for you. Now I must abandon you to your own devices. Your classmates will be back shortly to tidy up and change for dinner. I will leave you in their good hands."

Alone, Maureen looked around. The room was a corner one, with adjacent windows facing south and west. She leaned out of the south window, and found she was looking down onto the driveway. Beyond it a lawn sloped towards a burn that rippled along the low ground and vanished on the other side of an exotic-looking grove of bamboo to the right. Behind the burn the ground rose, gradually at first, then more steeply, its slopes crowded with trees and bushes, thinning gradually to heather-covered rocks. From the westerly window she could see Loch Kintray, a curved finger of the Atlantic prying into the rocky land, and, almost at the horizon, the hazy shadows of islands floating like clouds on the surface of the sea.

Outside, someone shouted and was answered. There was laughter. A whole group of girls was scrambling down the hill towards the burn. Some of them must be her form mates. Soon she would have to meet them, and here she was, hot, sweaty and disorganized. In a panic she bundled the contents of her cases into the drawers and wardrobe she had been assigned. Then she grabbed her sponge bag and towel and bolted into the relative privacy of the bathroom.

After a thorough washing she felt better and braver. *They can't kill me, after all*, she told herself firmly, as she walked back along the corridor and paused outside the Lower Fifth dorm. Her hand was on the doorknob when the conversation within made her freeze.

"Who is this person, anyway?"

"And why has she been put in with us?"

"What are we going to do, Kathleen? She'll spoil *everything*."

"Hush, Alison. We'll hold a council of war after dinner. In the bamboo grove. In the meantime be careful. Don't tell her anything."

Maureen backed away from the door and tiptoed down the passage. She slammed the bathroom door and walked back as noisily as it was possible to do in bedroom slippers. She took a deep breath and then, with a brave smile pasted on her face, she pushed open the door.

"Hello. My name's Maureen Frazer. I believe I'm to be in this dorm."

CHAPTER TWO

Maureen lay in an unfamiliar narrow bed, its lumpy mattress digging painfully into her spine below her shoulder blades. She moved cautiously, trying to find a more comfortable position. A shaft of white light poked through a gap in the curtains and fell across the four-poster. She could see the form prefect, Kathleen Buchanan, lying on her back with her black hair spread over the pillow, her dark eyelashes closed over eyes that were bluer than any Maureen had ever seen. She looked exactly the way Maureen wished she looked every time she examined herself in the mirror, to count the freckles on her cheekbones or to try to straighten the tangle of her bushy red hair.

Kathleen was in charge. There was no doubt about it. In the embarrassing moment when Maureen had introduced herself to the seven, it was Kathleen who had spoken, while the other six had stared silently at her. "You will be sleeping in that bed, Maureen. Fiona, you may share the four-poster with me, if you swear not to kick. If you do, I'll throw you out and choose someone else."

Then she had introduced the other six. Her voice was very "posh" and imperious. It reminded Maureen of old Lady Leith who, with her husband the judge, sat in the pew in front of them on Sundays.

Maureen watched the finger of moonlight trace a path across the room and went over the names in her head. There was Fiona Mackay, a plump girl with a tendency to giggle. Then there was Shelagh Drummond, who had almost smiled at her, as if friendship was a possibility. The others were Alison Watson, Eileen Kerr, Peggy Cowan and Moira Stewart, only she hadn't yet disentangled one from another. They had all looked at her with equally unwelcoming eyes. It doesn't matter, not knowing which is which, she told herself. Only one person counts, and that's Kathleen.

She had begun by bossing Maureen. "Do get those cases out of here. There isn't room to move."

"Please, where will I put them?"

"In the box room, of course. On the top floor. Just go up to . . . Oh, goodness, I suppose someone had better show you. You go, Shelagh, will you?"

Meekly Maureen had followed Shelagh, who had

a kind face and short, shiny brown hair, along the passage, up another flight of stairs and into a cupboard that surprisingly revealed more stairs ascending steeply to yet another floor.

"Here, give me one of those," Shelagh had offered, and they had hauled the cases into a round, dusty little room under the roof.

"Why, we're in one of the turrets, aren't we? What a great place for hide-and-seek or sardines."

Shelagh had chuckled. "My cousin Geoffrey stayed here once. He's twenty-two now and in the navy, on *Royal Oak*. But when he was little his father brought him to a house party here. He said they played Murder all over the lodge. That is, the grown-ups did. He was only allowed to watch."

"How unfair. Do you get to play Murder here? What fun it must be. I just love imagining things and pretending they're real, don't you?"

When Maureen had asked her that, Shelagh's cheerful expression had changed. It was very strange. Like a door being slammed in the face. "Miss Priestley doesn't encourage games in the house" was all she had said, but Maureen was left with the distinct impression that they *did* play something, something that her arrival had spoiled. "Don't tell her anything," Kathleen Buchanan had warned the others.

At dinner, under the watchful eyes of Miss Priestley and the other teachers, the seven Lower Fifth girls had been very polite to Maureen, passing her the butter, seeing that her water glass was filled. "And look out for the stew. It's rabbit, you know. The factor, MacDougall, shoots them. Last week Peggy nearly broke a tooth on a pellet."

When the pudding had arrived, a groan went up around the table. "Sally again!"

"Sally" was a shade of brilliant pink with no particular flavour, Maureen found.

"Sally-in-the-bath, you see," Moira—or perhaps it was Eileen—instructed her. "When it's chocolate it's called Sally-before-the-bath. Vanilla is Sally-after-the-bath."

"But Sally always tastes exactly the same," the others had chorused. In the laughter that followed Maureen saw Miss Priestley's approving eye on their table. The girls of the Lower Fifth were making the newcomer welcome.

Only they weren't. It was the kind of politeness that people might use with someone they hoped never to see again. It had an edge to it, and she felt more uncomfortable by the moment. Nothing had actually been said about her uniform, but they had all stared, and she felt second rate and shabby in last year's navy gym tunic, while all of them wore freshly laundered cream blouses and dark green well-fitting skirts. They tended to speak with what Maureen thought of as "posh" English accents, instead of comfortable east-coast Scottish ones, though she noticed that they slipped back if they got excited and forgot, especially Shelagh.

She's a jolly sort of person, Maureen thought.

Someone it would be nice to have as a friend. Not like Kathleen. Kathleen always had to be in charge, and she had a way of looking down her long straight nose with her chin tilted up, as if the person she was talking to was some inferior species like a beetle. But not when she spoke to the teachers. Then, Maureen noticed, she lowered her chin and her eyelids and became the model of a perfect young lady.

Och, it's all pretence, she thought. *I don't belong in an "academy for young ladies." I wish I were home with my own friends right now.* She was thankful, rather than offended, when dinner was over at last and Kathleen said firmly, "You must excuse us now. We have a project to finish."

She watched them walk decorously out of the panelled dining room and then, as if liberated from her, run down the hill towards the bamboo grove. She could hear them laughing and talking to each other. *Laughing at me,* she thought. *Glad to get away from me.*

"All alone?" Miss Priestley stopped beside her.

Maureen was tempted to ask the headmistress if she could sleep in the Lower Fourth dorm after all; but if she did, Miss Priestley would want to know why, and then Maureen would get the Lower Fifth into trouble. She certainly didn't want to do that. All she wanted was to be friends.

"I'm rather tired," she stammered. "It's been a long day."

"Indeed it has. An early night might be a good idea. Sleep well, my dear."

"Thank you, Miss Priestley."

So she was committed to going upstairs, undressing, washing, brushing her teeth and getting into bed in broad daylight. Lying in the horribly lumpy narrow bed, she listened to the clatter of feet on the stairs, the sound of voices and laughter, and felt lonelier than ever.

Eventually she had fallen asleep, only to wake up, hours later, to watch the pale moonbeam trace a path across the room. She listened to the breathing of the others, and began to imagine what was happening back in Saint Andrews. Mother would be tidying the house, packing, getting ready to board the London train. Daddy, handsome in his khaki uniform, had probably already sailed for France with the British Expeditionary Force. Both of them were going farther and farther away from her. She could still feel his arms hugging her goodbye, pressing her so hard against his chest that she could feel the imprint of his uniform buttons long after he had gone.

No more picnics together, she grieved. No more evenings sitting by the study fire reading quietly, now and then breaking the silence to say, "Oh, listen to this!" at some favourite passage. No more walks on a summer Sunday afternoon while Mother entertained her friends at tea.

"Now you wouldn't be pitying yourself, would you, child?" She could almost hear his voice. "Self-pity is a nasty habit, one that can drain all the courage out of your body."

"Be strong," he had said before he left.

"I will try. I really will," she had promised.

She sighed and turned over. *It is so bright, the moon must be nearly full*, she thought. *The same moon must be shining over Saint Andrews. Over our house. Over Daddy, wherever he is.* The lump in her chest grew heavier. It was a mistake thinking about them. No self-pity. She swallowed and shut her eyes tightly.

* * *

Breakfast of salty porridge and limp toast was followed by assembly, during which the blushing Maureen was introduced to the rest of the school. She told herself firmly that it wasn't too much of an ordeal, since only about fifty faces stared back at her instead of two hundred, as there would have been at her old school in Saint Andrews. But she knew the faces back home. She'd grown up with them all, played in the same streets, gone to the same church. These were all strangers, and unfriendly.

"Tell us something about yourself, dear," Miss Priestley encouraged.

Horror! Maureen gulped. She was sure she could see a smirk on Alison's face, and Moira's too. "I . . . I've lived all my life in Saint Andrews," she began and dried up.

"Yes?" Miss Priestley encouraged.

"And now Daddy—my father—he's been called up from the reserves and I suppose he's over in France by now. My mother is going into the Wrens. And I only have a granny in Edinburgh. So I got sent here," she finished in a rush, and then felt hot all over at the ungracious end to her statement. "I mean . . ." she stammered and stopped again.

Miss Priestley nodded. "Thank you, Maureen. You may sit down."

Maureen collapsed into her chair. Her blouse felt clammy under her arms and she prayed she wasn't going to get B.O. She wished she were invisible as well as odourless, but that was impossible. As she'd foreseen, she stuck out as "the new girl" in her navy tunic, while every other person wore green.

"As you know, girls," Miss Priestley went on smoothly, "school officially starts in four days. I'm sure you'll all be glad to settle into a regular routine once more." She smiled at the groan that went up. "But for the next few days we will continue to keep busy and useful. We hope to have hired full-time cleaning and kitchen staff after the weekend, but for the moment we must all pull our weight. Today the Upper and Lower Fourth will be on house duty: no skimping on mopping and dusting, please. The Upper and Lower Fifth may go up on the moor to gather blaeberries. MacDougall tells me there should still be plenty up there—if the magpies haven't taken them all. Do your best, girls, and I can promise you a change from Sally." She smiled.

"Imagine Miss Priestley knowing about Sally," Alison gasped as they made their way back to their dorm.

"Miss Priestley has eyes in the back of her head, and ears like a bat's," Kathleen snapped. "Fiona, smooth that side of the bedspread properly."

She was sitting on the windowsill, her arms circling her knees, while the other seven made their beds and tidied up. "That's why it's important for us to be very careful . . . about you-know-what," she added darkly.

Maureen felt herself turning red again. She punched her pillow vigorously and tucked her nightie under it. It was bad enough when they left her on her own. It was much worse when they referred to their secrets in front of her, as if she didn't count at all. As if she were invisible.

"That bed's a mess, Eileen. Do it again."

"I don't see why we should fuss," Eileen grumbled, but she obediently did as Kathleen told her. "Back home the servants did the cleaning up. Our parents pay large enough fees, after all."

"There's a war on," Alison mocked, and Eileen threw a pillow at her.

"Alison's right," Kathleen said. "We must take the long view. If our dorm is spotless, if we do everything better than anyone else, then Miss Priestley's not going to look too closely at how we use our spare time. Now, let's get some containers from the kitchen and go and pick more blaeberries than the Upper Fifth."

The path to the moor was no more than a rabbit trail, leading between low bushes and small trees up through increasingly steeper and rockier terrain. They walked in single file, almost in silence, with Kathleen naturally in the lead and Maureen trailing along in the rear. She was tempted to slow down until the others were out of sight and then find a hiding place, some-where overlooking the sea, where she could be alone, away from their barbs and their indifference. But she'd already been handed a basket, bigger than any of the others too. It was like a challenge. If she didn't fill it, they would probably blame her for not picking enough berries to avoid the dread Sally pudding. It would be another mark against her.

So she caught up with the others on top of the moor and, for a moment, forgot the misery that hung over her like a small black cloud. What a view! She turned round and round. To the north, far below, were the roofs of Kintray Lodge and, beyond them, planta-tions of dark pine and pale larch. Hills rolled away to Oban, somewhere up there, out of sight.

To the west the sea lay like a crinkled piece of sil-very silk. Today the islands of Scarba and Jura were as clear as if they'd been cut out of card, painted and set down on the water. To the south and east the moor-land stretched. Greedily Maureen took in the splen-dour, her heart pounding with excitement. This place was so different from the east coast and the bitter grey North Sea that it seemed a thousand miles away from the neat streets of Saint Andrews.

This was the country of *Kidnapped*. She could eas-ily imagine David Balfour coming ashore here, meet-ing again with Alan Breck Stewart, and running and hiding from the English soldiers . . .

Kathleen's voice brought her back to the present with a jolt.

"Let's go, girls. Watch your step. Look out for the boggy bits." She struck off in a southerly direction, with the others trailing along—*like sheep*, Maureen thought. She was about to tag reluctantly behind when Kathleen turned. "We'll do better if we spread out a bit. Maureen, why don't you go that way." She pointed to the east and Maureen obediently turned and walked along, her eyes on the ground, looking for blaeberry bushes. The breeze came off the sea, fresh and warm, carrying a scent of seaweed and bracken.

It also carried Kathleen's clear voice. "Hang on, the rest of you. Now that we're alone it's time for the Seven Magpies to have a conference."

Maureen told herself she didn't care. She didn't want to be part of their stupid secret society—or whatever it was. She picked over a patch of berries, then wandered on and found another, but the bushes grew sparsely and the berries barely filled the bottom of her basket. Unexpectedly she came upon a stretch of sphagnum moss, dry as white lace at its edges, brilliant green at its centre. When she tested it with her foot the ground shifted and moved under her, as if she were walking across a springy mattress. Scary, like quagmire. She jumped back and picked her way around the danger spot. Farther on, as the land sloped southwards, she found that the berries were juicier and more plentiful.

The rhythm of picking, of straightening her tired back and walking on, of bending and picking again, induced a kind of mindless trance. Maureen was vaguely aware of the soft air, of the buzzing of bees in a patch of heather, of the ache between her shoulder blades and the stickiness of her fingers. She picked until the basket was full, and only then did she slowly straighten up and look around.

There was not a soul in sight. Overhead a hawk soared, spied its prey somewhere over to the southeast and slipped downwards until it was out of sight below her. She strained her ears, but she could hear nothing but the thumping of her own heart. *Suppose I'm lost?* she thought, in a moment of panic. Then she told herself not to be silly. She looked at her watch. It was almost noon. So if she kept the southern sun just behind her left shoulder as she walked she would eventually arrive at that part of the moor that bordered the sea. Then she would have to turn north and find her way back to Kintray Lodge. Simple.

She set out briskly, came to another patch of bright green quaking bog and skirted it carefully. The ground was really wet around here. Perhaps she should turn back, go the other way; but that would take so long. Then she saw that to the south the ground fell away into a glen, with the bog water draining into a little burn that cascaded down the slope. She began to scramble downhill. The ground became firm beneath the grass and gradually more stony, so she could pick her way along without getting her shoes wet.

She came to the burn, clear and golden with peat. She washed her sticky hands, filled her palms and bent her head to drink. It was cold enough to make her teeth ache, but it had a clean sweet taste, quite unlike tap water. Along the edges of the burn the grass grew lushly. She should be able to jump across quite easily, so long as there were no stones hiding under the grass. It would be awful to twist an ankle out here, alone.

She pushed aside the heavy grass that drooped towards the water and then snatched her hand back as if it had been scalded. There, in the middle of the burn, as if it had been deliberately set in place, was a squared stone. But not a stepping stone. Carved on the south side, staring at her with blind, bulbous eyes, was a face. The golden water separated and rippled around the sides, then mingled again downstream. The burn's movement, reflected on the stone, made it seem as if the wide mouth was grinning at her.

Maureen's heart pounded. The sky was still and silent, the sun warm on her shoulders, but she felt cold. She could hear the thump, thump of her heart, and the sound of her breathing was loud in her ears. She reached out to the stone. Then she drew her hand back.

Had she any right to touch it? Had she any right to be here at all? Like a guardian of this place, the carving looked as ancient as the land itself. Who had made it and placed it in this secret burn? How long ago? And why?

The blind eyes stared at her, and the smiling mouth told her nothing. She shivered and looked up automatically. There was no cloud over the sun; just a hawk—

the same hawk?—endlessly circling. But there was something spooky about this place. She scrambled hastily to her feet and picked up the full basket of blaeberries. She wouldn't try to jump the burn here because the berries might spill. As for using the ancient head as a stepping stone—that was impossible.

Reluctantly she pulled her gaze away from those blind eyes. She slithered and slipped downhill until she came to a place where it was easier to cross. Then she turned and began the uphill trudge, the burn now on her right.

When she came to the secret place again she found herself stopping. If she hadn't known where the carved head lay under the concealing grass, she might never have seen it. The round blind eyes stared down the valley.

But she had seen the head, looked into those eyes, and somehow it seemed impossible just to turn her back on it. She couldn't just climb up the hill with her basket of blaeberries and join the others at the lodge for the ordinariness of sandwiches and apples.

Acknowledgement. Ceremony.

She remembered Daddy tossing a coin out of the car window as they drove across the Forth Bridge from Saint Andrews to Edinburgh to visit Gran. She'd been quite young then.

"Why did you do that, Daddy?" she'd asked, and he had grinned.

"Oh, just placating the old gods," he had said. "Rivers and streams are powerful forces in Celtic tradition."

She had nodded, satisfied.

"What nonsense!" Mother had said. "Sheer superstition! You shouldn't encourage the child."

Had Daddy thrown a coin every time they had crossed? Or only that one time that she remembered?

Now she found herself searching for a large flat leaf, scooping a handful of blaeberries onto it and placing it carefully on a stone that protruded into the burn like a small shelf, just below the head. It might almost have been placed there on purpose . . .

She stood and stretched. She felt wonderfully right, as if she were in tune with this strange new land. As if it had accepted her, the outsider. As if she were no longer an outsider.

She looked up the hill, suddenly afraid that the girls had been watching. *If Kathleen and the others had seen me do that, they'd think I was barmy*. But no one was in sight, and a glance at her watch told her that she was going to be late for lunch. She walked as fast as she could, dodging the wet bits and the patches of quagmire.

They could have waited for me, she thought crossly. *Suppose I had twisted my ankle down there by the burn. I could have lain there for days without being found*. A stupid thought, really. She knew that Miss Priestley would never allow one of her young ladies to go missing. But still, it was awfully unfriendly.

It wasn't long before she had climbed to the top of the moor again. Soon, to her relief, she was on familiar ground, the sea to her left, the hawk's-eye view of

Kintray Lodge below her. Almost immediately she heard voices.

"Maureen! Where are you?"

"Maureen!"

"Here I am," she called back.

They climbed up from among the trees to the north, their faces hot and red.

"Where on earth have you been?"

"Picking berries, of course." She showed them her full basket.

"We looked *everywhere*. You must have been hiding on purpose. It's too bad. We'll be hideously late for lunch and earn black marks, and it's all your fault."

It was obvious to Maureen that Kathleen had been really frightened and was making up for it by being extra furious. This didn't cow Maureen the way it would have done a few hours earlier. On the contrary, she felt a heady sense of power. She remembered the enigmatic smile on the stone face, accepting both her and her offering. She found herself smiling at Kathleen.

"I wasn't hiding," she said mildly. "Just picking berries."

"But we looked everywhere," Shelagh gasped. "Right over the top of the moor. Where did you go?"

Maureen was about to turn and point down towards the hidden burn, but she stopped herself. The carved head was *her* secret. The strange connection that had been forged between her and it, in the instant when she had offered it the berries, was private. The idea of those seven strangers charging down the hill, discovering the head, babbling about it, maybe even using it as a stepping stone, was unbearable.

She changed her pointing gesture into a wide sweep that embraced the whole southeast part of the moor. "There was a rabbit," she said vaguely.

Kathleen snorted. "There are a million rabbits, stupid. MacDougall shoots them by the dozen. Come on, then. We mustn't be any later than we need." She plunged down the track through the bracken and heather towards Kintray Lodge.

"I'll take the blame," Maureen shouted after her. "I'll say I wandered off and got lost."

"And have Miss Priestley blame me for not keeping an eye on you? No, thank you. You just be quiet and leave the explaining to me."

As they crossed the burn and climbed the slope of lawn towards the house, Kathleen suddenly stopped. "Here, Maureen, I'll take your basket."

"That's all right. I carried it all the way here. I can manage the rest of the way. It's not that heavy."

"Don't argue. Just do as you're told. Here, you can take mine." Kathleen quickly exchanged baskets and strode off across the driveway and into the house. Miss Priestley was lurking in the hall.

"Girls, where have you been? I was about to start a search party."

"Picking enough berries for a dozen tarts." Kathleen held out the heavy basket, filled to the brim. Her voice was as lighthearted as if she hadn't been in a rage the minute before.

"What a magnificent sight, Kathleen. Well done! If the rest of you have done as splendidly I am inclined to forgive your tardiness. But it mustn't happen again, or I shall have to restrict you to the gardens."

"Oh, it won't, Miss Priestley. We just got carried away."

"Very well. Take them through to the kitchen. Then wash your hands and hurry up with your lunch. It isn't fair to keep the cleaners-up waiting."

What a cheat Kathleen is, Maureen thought. *She and the others just play up to Miss Priestley, copying her manners and her way of speaking, instead of just talking with a normal Saint Andrews accent. It's all make-up, and I won't be part of it,* she told herself firmly, as she followed the others back into the dining room.

And I will keep my secret, she vowed.

After lunch the seven seemed to melt away, leaving Maureen alone. A little afraid of getting lost if she went out on her own, she began to explore the house, imagining it as it must have been in the pre-war days of shooting parties. Most of the large public rooms that must have been the drawing room, smoking room, morning room and so on were now classrooms, the desks lined up in neat rows ready for school to begin on Tuesday. Above were the dormitories. Some rooms had cards on their doors: Miss Priestley, Miss Urquhart, Miss Cavanagh and the other teachers. Each had the words **PRIVATE: NO ADMITTANCE** printed neatly above the name.

Slowly she went downstairs again and along another

corridor to discover the library. This was a magnificent room lined from floor to ceiling with shelves, the higher ones reached by a ladder that was fastened to a track below the uppermost shelf, so it could be scooted along the wall. For the most part, the books were leather-bound, dusty and ancient, looking as if they hadn't been touched in years. On a lower shelf near the door, how-ever, was a collection of bright covers. She crouched down to read the titles. Edgar Wallace. John Buchan. Agatha Christie. That was better.

She was just about to pick one off the shelf when she became aware of someone behind her. Miss Priestley, of course. What had Kathleen said? "Eyes in the back of her head and ears like a bat's."

Maureen scrambled to her feet. "Is it all right to read these, Miss Priestley?"

"They *are* the property of the laird, so I suppose I must hold them in trust. But these certainly don't look very valuable. Do you like reading?"

"I love it."

The headmistress smiled faintly. "Then I think it would be in order for you to borrow them." She paused, looking at Maureen with her head to one side. Then she nodded briskly. "I have a proposal. If you would like to undertake the job of dusting the shelves—and sorely do they need it—as payment you may borrow one book at a time. Is that a bargain?"

"Yes, thank you very much, Miss Priestley."

"You may begin now, if you wish. Go to the kitchen and ask for an apron and a duster. And white cotton gloves. They must have some stored away; the servants would have worn them for handling the silver in the old days."

It certainly wasn't the most exciting way to spend a day, but it was better than sitting around looking like an extra thumb. For the rest of the afternoon Maureen lifted books from the shelves, dusted them thoroughly and put them back. Many of the titles were in Latin and some were collections of sermons, as dry as the dust that covered them. She couldn't imagine anyone curling up in one of the big leather chairs to read them, and she said as much to Miss Priestley when the headmistress returned to see how the work was going.

Miss Priestley laughed. "I imagine that hunting parties didn't have a very high proportion of avid readers. My guess is that most of these were bought as a job lot to fill the shelves."

Maureen had never heard of books being bought by the yard like wallpaper. "How awful!"

"If you do find something interesting, make sure you take your gloves off before reading. I see they are already quite soiled."

"Yes, Miss Priestley."

"And don't spend all your time cooped up in here. I didn't intend to turn you into a slave."

"But I like it. It's peaceful in here."

"Hmm." Miss Priestley skewered her with a look that made her squirm. "You *are* settling down all right, aren't you? Getting on well with your classmates?"

"I'm just grand, Miss Priestley, thank you. Honestly."

She looked unflinchingly into the headmistress's eyes as she lied.

* * *

On Saturday they had to help their form mistress, Miss Urquhart, sort out boxes of textbooks. After that there was tennis, and on Sunday a quiet walk and letter writing. It wasn't until the following Monday that Maureen was able to return to the library.

I'm not lonely, she told herself firmly. It was lonelier having to play tennis with Alison and Moira and Peggy, her partner sighing heavily any time she missed a serve; and it was even worse tagging along on the Sunday walk. She finished dusting a row of sermons and began on a more interesting shelf with books about the history of the Highlands, which she promised herself she would read sometime, and with a couple of books on the Celtic tradition in Scotland.

One of these, marked with an ancient train ticket, fell open at a page headed "The Cult of the Severed Head." She almost fell off the ladder with excitement. She climbed down and, remembering Miss Priestley's instructions, peeled off her soiled gloves. She took the book over to one of the leather armchairs, fragrant with the memory of old cigar smoke, and began to read.

> In Celtic times, the head was considered
> the seat of the soul, the essence of being.
> It symbolized the divine; it possessed all

> desirable qualities. People believed that
> the spirit lingered in the head, even after
> the death of the body, and it could avert
> evil as well as prophesy. Carved repre-
> sentations of the Severed Head presided
> over the feasts of the Otherworld.

Maureen suddenly shivered, remembering the
apparition of the severed head in *Macbeth*, which
they'd studied the year before in her Saint Andrews
school. She went on reading.

> Hundreds of carved stone heads have
> been discovered across Britain, espe-
> cially in the west and north. In all cases
> they have enormous eyes, signifying
> their ability to see all: to prophesy. Even
> today some isolated inhabitants of
> North Britain acknowledge the "power"
> of these stone heads with offerings of
> flowers or food.

And somehow I knew that, Maureen thought. *I gave
it blaeberries*. How strange! She closed the book and
stared out of the window in amazement. What she had
done was more than just acting a part, more than the
kind of imagining that had made her pretend to be
David Balfour, hiding from his enemies in the Scottish
highlands. That was *almost* real while she was imagining it, but not afterwards.

Her response to the discovery of the stone head had been altogether different. The offering of blaeberries was much more than a game. And now she understood why. The feeling of being accepted, the rightness of what she had done, was all *real*. It was as if a door into another, and until now, unbelievable world had swung open.

* * *

She couldn't stop thinking about the blind-eyed head all through dinner and recreation, and when she woke up suddenly in the middle of the night to see the full moon stream across the room it was still there in her mind, staring at her with bulging eyes.

She turned over and tried to go to sleep again, but thoughts of Daddy, of Mother, now in her naval uniform, and of the secrets that her form mates were keeping from her, kept getting in the way. She lay listening to the quiet breathing of the others. Somewhere in the moonlit world outside an owl hooted.

Maybe if she had a drink of water she'd be able to get back to sleep. She wriggled quietly out of bed and tiptoed from the room in her bare feet. As she passed the four-poster she could see Kathleen sprawled on her back, her black hair spread over the pillow. Of Fiona there was no sign. Probably gone to the lav, Maureen thought, feeling her way along the corridor, which was lit only by traces of moonlight. Perhaps that was what had wakened her. But Fiona wasn't there.

On her way back to bed a tall dark shadow loomed up in front of her, and her heart suddenly jumped. Nobody had said anything about ghosts, but in an old house like this they were certainly possible. She shrank against the wall, her knees suddenly weak. Then the brilliant beam of light from a torch dazzled her and her hand went automatically up to her eyes. She let out her breath in a sigh of relief. *Ghosts don't carry torches*, she told herself, and whispered, "Who's there?"

"This is Miss Cavanagh. More to the point, who are you? Why, it's the new girl, Maureen Frazer, isn't it?"

"Yes, Miss Cavanagh."

"What are you doing wandering around in the middle of the night, Maureen? You must know that is not acceptable behaviour."

"I just went for a drink of water, Miss Cavanagh."

"Nonsense. I distinctly heard footsteps on the main stairs."

Maureen opened her mouth to deny the accusation. Then into her mind flashed the picture of the empty pillow beside Kathleen's. Fiona. She remembered the words she had overheard that first day: *What'll we do? She'll spoil everything*. Whatever the Lower Fifth were up to, it was her responsibility as a form member— however despised—to cover up for them, to protect Fiona.

"I . . . I got muddled," she stammered. "I couldn't remember where the bathroom was."

"After four days here?" The teacher didn't sound convinced. "Well, off to bed with you now. Remember, school starts tomorrow. Try not to disturb anyone else. I, for one, am a very light sleeper." It sounded like a threat.

Maureen pushed the half-opened door wide and tiptoed back to her bed. She could have sworn that Kathleen's eyes were open. They glinted in the moonlight as she tiptoed past the four-poster, but Kathleen said nothing. Fiona had still not returned. Where could she be? Maureen climbed into bed, pulled the blanket over her head and finally went back to sleep.

CHAPTER THREE

It was a relief when school started on the nineteenth of September. The four days before had been a kind of holiday, but rather a miserable one without Mother and Daddy or a single friend to have fun with. Now the days would have a shape to them, and Maureen knew where she was supposed to be and what she was supposed to be doing—sitting at a regular desk in her form and studying from familiar books, even if the room had once been the bedroom of the laird's wife, its walls covered with rosebud wallpaper.

She discovered with relief, on that first day, that she was at least as clever as Kathleen and Alison, and a lot cleverer than the others. Thank goodness she wouldn't be shown up as stupid. *Why, my school is every bit as good as the Logan Academy for Young Ladies*, she thought. In maths she usually got ten out of ten, running neck and neck with Alison.

"Aha, some competition at last," Miss Urquhart had teased, and Alison's pale face had turned red.

This suggestion that Maureen was "competition" was embarrassing, and certainly didn't help her status as the Outsider. Nor did the essay assignment that Miss Urquhart set them in the first week of school. The topic was "My Favourite Person."

Easy, Maureen thought and wrote lovingly about her father, their walks and talks and reading together. She had summed up their relationship in the last paragraph of her essay: "He has taught me to be my own person, not to be afraid to question the opinions of others, if I should feel them not to be right. I owe him so much."

Miss Urquhart had read her essay out loud to the whole class, while Maureen sat staring at her desk, not wanting to meet the disdainful glare of the others, feeling her cheeks getting hotter and hotter. Worst of all, Miss Urquhart had then criticized Kathleen's effort, which she said was "ill thought-out and sloppily composed."

Her good work certainly didn't make Maureen's relationship with her form mates any more comfortable, but at least while they were all occupied in class she wasn't as aware of her loneliness. Then in her spare time she took herself off to the library, ignoring the whispered allusions to the "Seven Magpies."

Curiously she riffled through the other books on Scottish history. While she didn't find anything else as exciting as the explanation of the stone heads, a photograph in one of the books had brought back the memory of the hidden stone in the burn so strongly that she got the shivers. The blank eyes seemed to be saying something to her—something mysterious, even though she couldn't understand the silent message.

* * *

"Lower Fifth, I'd like you to take a message down to the factor's house," Miss Priestley said after assembly the next Saturday. "That includes you too, Maureen. You can't spend all day cooped up in the library. Some fresh air will do you good."

It was a glorious day. Blinking in the brilliant sunshine, Maureen felt like Mole coming out of his hole to find spring. "What are you standing there for with that funny expression on your face?" Kathleen asked irritably. Maureen thought her form mates would make fun of her if she told them. *They* probably didn't read books like *The Wind in the Willows*, and they'd think she was an awful baby because she still loved it. She said nothing.

"Well, come on then," Kathleen said impatiently. "And try not to get lost this time."

"I wasn't lost before," Maureen retorted.

"So the cat gave you back your tongue?" Kathleen spun round and glared at her, her bright blue eyes hard as sapphires. "What *were* you up to on the moor then, Maureen Frazer?"

"Nothing." In spite of herself, Maureen felt her cheeks get hot. *There's no way I'm going to tell you about the head in the burn*, she told herself firmly. *That's my secret, not yours*. But she didn't say this out loud.

Kathleen tossed her head and ran down the path through the rhododendron thicket. Maureen slowly followed the other girls, thinking, *I won that round, anyhow!* But the knowledge didn't make her any happier.

Off the main track a path branched leftwards towards the rough meadowland, and it was here, above the ancient seashore, that the MacDougall cottage stood. It was a tiny stone house roofed with slate, its narrow windows curtained against the magnificence of the view. Maureen wondered if, perhaps, the hugeness of the landscape might grow to be overwhelming, seen day in and day out for a lifetime.

Mrs. MacDougall met them at the door, wiping her hands on her apron. She reminded Maureen of the woman on the train, her face weather-beaten, her grey hair wound into a bun so tight that it was a wonder the hairpins would go through it at all. Her hands were red, the knuckles swollen and chapped.

"Och, it's you then," she said abruptly when she saw Kathleen, who was in front. Her eyelids drooped, reminding Maureen of a bird of prey, a hawk maybe.

"Yes, it's us, Mrs. MacDougall," Kathleen said

brightly in her posh "English" voice. "May we come in? Miss Priestley sent us down with a message."

"Oh, aye? Well . . . I suppose you may as well. Come away in then."

It was a grudging kind of welcome, not what Maureen expected. She'd always heard that Highlanders were very hospitable. Even if Kintray Lodge *was* twenty miles south of Loch Linnhe, the factor's wife had a voice with a true Highland lilt. She got the impression that Mrs. MacDougall disliked Kathleen. Perhaps it was just the prefect's bossy manner and the behaviour of the others. They all elbowed their way into the tiny room and looked around as if it were an exhibit in a museum, not the private home of the factor and his wife. Nobody bothered to introduce Maureen, so she went up to Mrs. MacDougall and held out her hand. "We've not met before, Mrs. MacDougall. I'm Maureen Frazer."

Her hand was taken, reluctantly at first, but then it was held with a firmer pressure, and Mrs. MacDougall's left hand came up to cover it. The woman's blue eyes seemed to pierce hers. Then she nodded. "Maureen Frazer. Aye. You're welcome, lass."

It was only a handshake, but Maureen had the weird feeling that something tremendous had just happened, like two old friends recognizing each other. The ordinary word "welcome" seemed to carry its old meaning of "well come," and the same feeling of belonging that Maureen had felt down at the burn swept over her again.

But there was no time for more than a smile. Kathleen held out the envelope from Miss Priestley, Mrs. MacDougall dropped Maureen's hand and the spell was broken.

Maureen looked appreciatively at the cosy room. In the middle was a wooden table, scrubbed silver white, with four chairs around it. To the left a wood-burning stove shone with black lead. Shelves stacked with coarse blue and white pottery covered the back wall above a stone sink. In front of the peat fire was a wooden settle and on the mantel above the fire a series of photographs, obviously of the MacDougall family. A golden coin lay in front of them, and a cross-stitched sampler hung on the wall above.

The sampler had the motto I KNOW THEIR SOR-ROWS, with a border of ivy leaves around it. It was signed ELSPETH SHAW, AGED TEN and dated JUNE 14, 1856. Above the ivy leaves, as if it had just alighted there, was a single perky black-and-white magpie.

"That's weird," she said aloud. "I've never seen a magpie in a sampler before. It's not exactly a pretty bird, is it?"

"'Tis a telling bird. 'One for sorrow', you ken."

"I don't know . . ."

"You've no heard of the seven magpies then?"

Seven Magpies? Was the factor's wife part of the secret society? *No, that's ridiculous*, Maureen told herself and, as she shook her head, she had the odd feeling that the other girls in the room had drawn together, that they were holding their breaths, waiting for what she was going to say.

"No, I've not heard of them."

There was a sigh, as if seven people had exhaled at once. "Come on," said Kathleen briskly. "Time we were going. Good morning to you, Mrs. MacDougall."

"Good morning, young ladies." The factor's wife nodded gravely, dismissing them. But as Maureen followed the others out, the woman grasped her wrist. "One for sorrow, you ken," she whispered. "And two for—"

"Come on, Maureen," Kathleen called from outside.

"I must go. Thank you. May I come and see you another time?"

"Alone, aye. Not with *them*. Come for tea."

"May I? Next Saturday, perhaps? If I can get away. Thank you."

She ran to catch up with Shelagh, who was lagging a few steps behind the other girls. "What an interesting woman. What d'you suppose she meant—the telling bird?"

Before Shelagh could answer, Kathleen turned round. "She's just an old country woman, full of stories. Meaningless, really."

"'I know their sorrows'," Maureen quoted. "And a single magpie on the sampler. 'One for sorrow'. I wonder why?"

"Oh, go look it up in your old library, why don't you, and stop boring us to death."

Maureen felt her cheeks get pink. "All right, I will."

Let them go ahead and do whatever they want to do, she told herself firmly. *I don't care. I don't mind being alone. I've got my own secret.* But, even while she thought it, she knew in her heart that a secret was a poor substitute for real friends.

Telling herself she didn't care a pin, she ran back to the lodge, got her apron and duster and returned to her task of cleaning the library books, keeping an eye out for anything about Highland superstitions and magpies. But all she found were some yellowed theatre tickets, an old cutting from *The Scotsman* and a couple of letters. She was tempted to read them, but told herself that they were none of her business and tucked them back inside their books. Seeing them made her wonder how long it would be before she got letters of her own, from Mother and from darling Daddy in France—would he be allowed to write? She sighed and went on dusting until the lunch bell rang.

* * *

The very next Monday there was a letter from Mother, giving a temporary Wren address and enclosing a tin of sweets and a package of shortbread, but no real news. Maureen thought of the presents as guilt offerings, to make up for Maureen's being stuck out on the west coast of Scotland while Mother had all the fun in London. She shared the sweets with the other girls, who took them reluctantly and were no nicer to her than before.

The next Saturday Maureen slipped out of the lodge after lunch, taking with her the package of shortbread. She walked alone through the dark grove of rhododendrons and across the stubbly grass to the factor's cottage.

Mrs. MacDougall opened the door at once, almost as if she'd been expecting her. Maureen told herself not to be so imaginative. Probably the factor's wife had simply glanced out of the window and seen her coming down the path. Yet it had felt like magic, like the beginning of a folktale—in which anything might happen.

She was alone, for which Maureen was thankful. She was rather intimidated by the factor, whom she'd seen about the place, tending to the estate, felling old trees, bringing rabbits up to the lodge kitchen for dinner. He was a dour man, with a long face, tight lips and reddish hair turning white. She felt he didn't like the girls being there—or maybe he was just shy.

"Come away in." Mrs. MacDougall held the door wide. "I've just wetted the tea."

With a smile Maureen offered the package of shortbread, which was accepted with a gracious nod, as between equals. "McVitie and Price? Aye, they make a bonny biscuit. Sit you down and I'll mash the tea."

Seated at the newly scrubbed table, Maureen watched Mrs. MacDougall briskly stir the tea, set the shortbread on a platter commemorating the Silver Jubilee and pour.

"Milk?"

"Yes, please."

"Sugar?"

"N-no, thank you." Maureen liked her tea sweet, but they had already been warned by Miss Priestley that sugar would soon be in short supply.

"A wee teaspoon, surely?" Mrs. MacDougall urged.

"Well, thank you. If you're sure . . ."

"You didna come to the lodge with the other young ladies, did you?"

Maureen shook her head and, between sips of tea and bites of shortbread, she explained.

Mrs. MacDougall sat quietly and listened. *She has a listening face*, thought Maureen. *Like Gran.* A flood of homesickness for Daddy and Mother and her Edinburgh gran swept over her. Before she knew it she was pouring out the whole story of why she was here, and how snooty the girls in her form were. She was astonished when the little clock on the mantel chimed four.

"Goodness, I must go. Mrs. MacDougall, this is awful. I've done nothing but talk about myself the whole afternoon. I've never even asked after *your* family."

The factor's wife smiled. "The happenings of young people are a deal more interesting than those of us old folks. Come again, will you now?"

"Oh, I will. Thank you."

Her hand on the door latch, she turned. "I completely forgot. The rhyme about the telling birds—the magpies?"

"Oh, aye." The woman stood with her hands folded over her apron and recited gravely:

> One for Sorrow
> Two for Joy
> Three for a Girl
> Four for a Boy
> Five for Silver
> Six for Gold
> Seven for a secret that can ne'er be told.

A shiver ran down Maureen's back. "Thank you," she stammered, and began to run up the slope towards the lodge. There was something magical in those words, something that made the hair prickle on her arms. *Seven for a secret that can ne'er be told.* An incantation. Like the carved head in the burn, the rhyme was part of the same magic, wasn't it? *But what on earth does it have to do with the secret society of the Lower Fifth?* As she walked alone across the great hall, she wondered if she would ever find out.

Being sucked back into the Saturday routine of study, dinner and music was a shock—like being dragged out of a good book at the most exciting moment.

"So where've you been all afternoon, pray tell?" Kathleen quizzed her as they tidied for dinner.

"Nowhere particular," Maureen said vaguely. Mrs. MacDougall was *her* friend, just as the carved head was *her* secret.

"What do you have to be so secretive about?" Alison teased, uncannily echoing Maureen's thoughts. "Oh, look, girls. She's blushing." The others laughed and Maureen felt her cheeks growing hotter.

"Och, why don't you leave her be," Shelagh interrupted. "What do you expect her to be doing while we're talking about—"

"Talking about nothing in particular," Kathleen said, cutting her off icily. "Where's your loyalty, Shelagh?"

"Yes, where, Shelagh?" Peggy and Moira chorused.

Even in the midst of her embarrassment, Maureen noticed how the seven girls, who had seemed so alike at first in their green and gold uniforms, really had such different personalities. Peggy and Moira were best chums; they'd lived on the same street in Saint Andrews all their lives, and they never seemed to have an independent thought. Alison was very different. Maureen sometimes wondered why *she* wasn't the leader. She was certainly as smart as Kathleen and much quicker in class. Perhaps it had to do with the kind of family Kathleen came from, something that gave her the instinctive right to boss the others.

But there's more to it than that, Maureen thought. *Maybe something to do with those Seven Magpies.*

Sunday dragged by. It was always a slow day at the lodge, while at home it had always been such fun. After church Daddy would sometimes persuade Mother to leave her committee paperwork and take a picnic into the country. When Mother relaxed—which wasn't often—she could be almost as much fun as Daddy.

The problem with Sunday at the lodge was that it came before Monday, and *Monday* was one of the days when the post van went from Oban to Lochgilphead and dropped the post off at the lodge. Everyone waited and longed for Mondays.

After they arrived, the letters were sorted by Miss Priestley and then handed over to the form mistresses to distribute. Gran's letters were the longest and most interesting that Maureen received. Today's was full of cosy chat about how the fishmonger would no longer give her free scraps for Ginger, and how cigarettes were getting hard to come by, unless you had a regular supplier who would keep some aside for you. She said she had given up sugar in her tea and was saving what she could put aside for jam-making next summer. Maureen stared at the letter in dismay. *Next summer!* The war was supposed to be over before the summer. Everyone said so.

There was a slim form letter from Daddy, saying he was well and loved her, but with no news at all. *It would be censored*, Maureen supposed. And from Mother a quick scrawl with her new address, "HMS Pembroke," which didn't mean a ship at all but was just a forwarding address to some unknown place on dry land.

Darling,

Not a minute to myself. We are busy organizing—all hush-hush, of course.

Had dinner at the Savoy with John
Pinkney. You wouldn't think there was a
war on with the food there. I don't know
how they do it. Divine piano player to
dance to.

Love, Mother.

Maureen stared bleakly at the letter, trying to read
between the lines. Who was John Pinkney? And why
was Mother dancing with him, with Daddy somewhere in France maybe risking his life?

Oh, Mother, she wanted to say. *Don't forget Daddy.
Don't have too good a time.*

Her thoughts were interrupted by Kathleen's carrying voice. "Darlings, imagine! Cousin Imogen is going
to marry the Honourable Basil Thwaite, of all people.
What a joke!"

To Maureen, Kathleen sounded like someone out of
a Noel Coward comedy, but Peggy and Moira chorused their enthusiasm and Fiona joined in. Alison
looked up from her letter and said, "Who, Kathleen?"
then went back to reading without waiting for an
answer.

Shelagh, looking through a sheaf of snapshots,
wasn't paying attention. When she caught Maureen
looking at her, Maureen blushed. "Sorry. But you do
have a lot of letters."

"Aren't I lucky? Besides Mummy and Daddy, there's
my two sisters and all the aunts and uncles and
cousins. D'you want to look?"

"I'd love to." Maureen looked through the snaps, at faces that mirrored Shelagh's smile and freckles, at new babies looking like—well, like new babies. One picture was of a young man in his early twenties, in lieutenant's uniform.

"Goodness, he's good-looking," Maureen gasped.

"Geoff Drummond? He's my top favourite cousin." Shelagh beamed.

"Who are these others?"

"Och, you wouldn't want to know. You'd be bored."

"Of course I wouldn't be."

"Are you sure now? The other girls—"

"Tell me about them," said Maureen firmly, and shut out Kathleen's piercing voice so she could hear Shelagh's family history.

How nice to belong to a big family, she thought, with just the smallest twinge of envy. *To have all these people to love, and who love you. We're so small a family, us Frazers, almost nonexistent. Gran and Daddy. Mother and me. But it's enough when there's love*, she told herself firmly. *Gran and Daddy, yes. Only there's a kind of brittleness about Mother that makes her hard to touch. But her committees think she's wonderful and I bet her Wrens do too. They'll probably get crushes on her.*

Then Miss Urquhart told them to put their letters away, that it was time to resume lessons. Physical geography and the effects of the Ice Age. In the afternoon she took them down to the shore and pointed out the raised glacial beaches that were terraced at twenty-five and a hundred feet above the sea. These beaches were evidence, she told them, of how the land rose as the ice front retreated. "As recently as ten thousand years ago, young ladies, when primitive man was hunting the mammoth and the reindeer in Europe."

"Were humans living here then?" Maureen asked, remembering the stone head and wondering how long ago it had been carved and set in the burn. For how long had people been giving it offerings of fruit and flowers? Was it the original head? Or, as it had worn out through the centuries, had someone lovingly remade it in the same image?

"That's a good question, Maureen." Miss Urquhart nodded approvingly. "No, the ice didn't retreat from northern Britain until about six thousand B.C.— almost eight thousand years ago. But since that time this area has always been inhabited. There are neolithic burial sites in the neighbourhood. Perhaps in the spring we will make an expedition to some of them."

"Oh, yes!" Maureen glowed.

"Are you interested in archaeology?"

"I don't know much about it, Miss Urquhart."

"Boring, boring. Why don't you hush up?" Fiona muttered under her breath.

Maureen blushed and moved away from Miss Urquhart's side. It was bad enough to be the form outsider. Far worse to be caught sucking up to the teacher.

Miss Urquhart looked at her watch. "Time for tea, girls."

As they broke into a run, she called them back. "Steady, girls. One moment, if you please. As an English assignment you will write an essay on the effects of the Ice Age on the topography of western Scotland."

Eileen groaned. "But we don't know anything about it."

Miss Urquhart looked at her. "Really, sometimes I despair! If you had been paying any attention to me, Eileen Kerr, you would have plenty of material." She turned to the rest of the form. "You will be marked on both your understanding of the subject and your English construction."

"That's not fair," Peggy and Moira muttered.

Kathleen frowned at them. "If we didn't catch everything you said, we'll find books in the library, won't we?"

"I'm sure you will. Perhaps Maureen will help you locate useful material. You also have your text on physical geography to jog your failing memories." With that Miss Urquhart strode up the path through the rhododendrons.

Kathleen glared at Peggy, Moira and Eileen. "What's the matter with you three? If you annoy her you'll start getting bad marks. Remember what we decided when we arrived here? Perfect behaviour. Then they'll leave us alone to get on with our own activities in our spare time with no questions asked. As for you, Maureen Frazer, I'll thank you not to show off like that again. You make the others look bad."

"Och, it was just a question," Shelagh blurted out. "You're no being fair, Kath."

Kathleen looked taken aback. Then she smiled. "I don't mean to be unfair, Shelagh. But Maureen has to be careful. She doesn't know our ways yet."

And I wonder if I ever will. Maureen followed the others up to the lodge for tea and scones, with very little butter and only a scraping of jam. She wondered how Shelagh got away with criticizing Kathleen when none of the others dared. Alison was too like Kathleen herself, perhaps, and Fiona had a crush on her. But the others? You'd think they'd show some spunk. Again the secret of the Seven Magpies teased her. Was it the secret society that gave Kathleen her hold over them?

"Thanks for standing up for me," she whispered to Shelagh as they went back to their classroom for study time.

Shelagh grinned. "That's fine. She's all right really. It's just that being prefect tends to go to her head a bit."

Being prefect? Was that all it was? Maureen wasn't convinced. But with that answer she had to be satisfied.

CHAPTER FOUR

The weeks formed a kind of rhythm. Sunday was always letter-writing day. On Mondays, Wednesdays and Fridays the post van came from Oban. Miss Urquhart kept them working hard towards their Junior Certificate. The evenings began to grow cool and the nights were brilliant with stars. Not a light was allowed to show from the lodge or the factor's cottage. Once in a while the wardens would drive down from Oban to check the blackout, particularly in those houses that overlooked the sea.

Though the plantations of pines remained dark and dour, the larches turned gold. Otherwise there was little to mark one week from the next. Miss Priestley had *The Scotsman* delivered from Oban, and the teachers had a wireless in their sitting room. But hardly any of this news filtered down to the students.

It was almost hypnotic how time went by. Maureen studied very hard and tried not to allow the secret meetings in the bamboo grove to bother her. "Bleak, but bearable" was how she would have defined her life, if asked; but she could not breathe a word of that in her letters, not even to Gran. Letters had to be light and amusing and, since she had been warned that they were scanned by Miss Priestley's eagle eye before being posted, they could contain no secrets.

"Oh, do look," Shelagh said to her, one Wednesday in mid-October. "Here's my latest nephew. Isn't he grand?" She passed the snaps to Maureen, who couldn't help smiling at the bright-faced baby.

"Oh, he's *sweet*. You *are* lucky being an aunt. That's something that'll never happen to me, being an 'only'." She passed the pictures back just as Shelagh was opening another letter. She saw the paper quiver between Shelagh's fingers and her face go white.

"What is it? What's happened?" she hissed, but at that moment Miss Urquhart looked at her watch.

"Put away your correspondence now, girls. Time for English. Open your poetry book at page 428. Kathleen, begin reading, please."

Kathleen stood up and began to recite, using her most "Englishy" voice. But the poem was an old Scottish one, *The Ballad of Sir Patrick Spens*, and Maureen thought it sounded dreadful read that way. So, apparently, did Miss Urquhart.

"Stop, stop! Where is your feeling, Kathleen? This is a *tragic* story. No, you may sit down. Maureen, you read it."

Horribly aware of Kathleen's angry eyes boring into her, Maureen stood up and began to read. But the poem was one of her favourites and before long she forgot Kathleen and read with gusto, the old Scots words rolling off her tongue. In the story the king had ordered his favourite knight to sail to Norway to bring back the princess to wed his son, even though it was a dangerous season for sailing. Right away the trouble had begun.

> They hadna sailed a league, a league,
> A league but barely three,
> When the lift grew dark, and the wind blew loud,
> And gurly grew the sea.

As she imagined the sky darkening and the swell of the sea growing more violent, Maureen was transported by the words. No longer was she standing by her desk with the blue-bound book of verse in her hands and Kathleen glaring at her from the next desk. She was with brave Sir Patrick Spens on the quarterdeck of his doomed ship. He struggled safely through the storms to Norway, and was homeward bound with the princess aboard when the masts snapped and the waves engulfed the ship.

> And lang, lang, may the maidens sit
> Wi' their gowd kames in their hair,

A-waiting for their ain dear loves!
For them they'll see nae mair.
Half-oure, half-oure to Aberdour,
'Tis fifty fathoms deep;
And there lies guid Sir Patrick Spens,
Wi' the Scots lords at his feet!

As the last words rolled off Maureen's tongue, while she was still imagining the maidens weeping for their lost lords, the gold combs in their hair, she was startled by a sudden wail. The book clattered to the floor. In the desk next to hers, Shelagh jumped to her feet, pushing aside her chair so violently that it scratched across the polished floor.

"Gently," Miss Urquhart began, and then stopped as Shelagh gave a choking sob and ran out of the room, leaving the door ajar behind her.

"My goodness!" Miss Urquhart rose, putting a marker in her book. "Read on quietly until I return, girls."

"What was that all about, Kathleen?" Alison whispered.

Kathleen shrugged. "Nothing to do with *me*."

"It was a letter," Maureen said. "I think it was bad news."

"How would *you* know?"

Maureen swallowed her reply and sat staring at the next ballad, by "anonymous." The words floated across the page, refusing to be pinned down and made sense of. What terrible news had been contained in

Shelagh's letter? Poor Shelagh. And to think Maureen had just been envying her—

"Maureen!" She looked up with a start to see Miss Urquhart in the doorway, beckoning to her. Once Maureen had joined her outside, she whispered, "Shelagh has had bad news. She doesn't want a fuss made, but she said she would prefer to remain out of class for the rest of the afternoon. When I told her that I felt she should not be alone, she asked if you might be allowed to join her."

"Me? Are you sure, Miss Urquhart? Not Kathleen?"

"No. She specifically asked that *you* might accompany her. Perhaps you would like to walk along the shore. It's a pleasantly warm day. But do not stray too far from the house, and please make note of the time to be sure you're back before dinner. It'll be getting dusk by then, of course, won't it? So watch the time."

"Yes, Miss Urquhart." Maureen went up to the dorm to get a cardigan and picked up one for Shelagh as well. Then she walked slowly downstairs, wondering what to say, what to do. She'd never had to face tragedy in real life—only in novels.

Shelagh was standing in the hall by the main door, her face puffy and blotched, her eyes swollen. She looked a mess.

I expect that's why she wanted me, Maureen told herself. *I don't matter, so she won't mind me seeing her like this.*

"Thanks for chumming me."

"That's all right," Maureen said awkwardly. "I brought a cardigan. You'd better put it on."

Shelagh looked blankly at the sweater, but she let Maureen help her into it. Then they walked silently down the driveway towards the sea. The rhododendrons were dark and gloomy, and the earth smelt damp and bitter. *Like an old cemetery*, Maureen thought. She shivered and pulled her cardigan across her chest. It was hard to imagine that in six months or so this driveway would be a mass of brilliant flowers. But it would be so. She wished that she could comfort Shelagh with this thought—that winter *would* give way to spring, and that maybe whatever awful thing had happened might not be so bad later on. But she didn't know how to put this into words. They tramped along until the silence became unbearable.

"Who was the letter from?" she asked abruptly.

"Mummy. About cousin Geoff."

"The one in the navy? The one who stayed here when he was little, when they all played Murder?"

Shelagh nodded. "He's my favourite cousin. I mean, he *was*." She stopped and mopped her eyes.

"You mean he's . . ." Maureen stopped and swallowed. "Oh, Shelagh, I didn't think the war was actually beginning to happen yet. Not *here*."

"Neither did I. It doesn't seem real, does it? Geoff was on the battleship *Royal Oak*. Up at Scapa Flow. It was blown up at its moorings by a U-boat that sneaked into the harbour in the middle of the night. Geoff was duty officer. They phoned my aunt."

Scapa Flow. The safest of safe harbours, nestled in the Orkney Islands off the north of Scotland. *Safe?* With German submarines lurking, penetrating its defences? And the Orkneys were not so many miles away either. Not by sea.

All these ideas hurtled around in her head as she impulsively caught hold of Shelagh's hand. It felt cold and damp, and Maureen would rather have let go, but she made herself hold on, trying to will the warmth out of her own hand into the other. Shelagh held on tightly, so maybe it was some kind of comfort.

They came out into the sunlight and walked down towards the shore. The gentle waves sparkled cheerfully as if nothing were wrong, as if the girls were there for the holidays instead of for the Duration. The sea looked safe and innocent—not as if a battleship were lying in pieces at its bottom, blasted out of existence by an enemy submarine.

And there lies guid Sir Patrick Spens, wi' the Scots lords at his feet. Maureen stopped suddenly and let go of Shelagh's hand. She could feel the hot blush spread from her neck to her cheeks, and she put her hands over them.

"Och, Shelagh, what an awful thing I did!"

"What do you mean?"

"Reading that poem the very minute after you got the letter from your mother. I didn't know."

"Of course you didn't. It wasn't your fault, silly. It was Miss Urquhart's choice."

"Still . . ."

"It's all right. Dinna fash yourself about it." Shelagh spoke in comfortable Scots, not even pretending to use the Logan Academy accent. Maureen felt less awkward.

"You're sure?"

"Of course I am, dafty."

They walked southwards along the shore, automatically stamping the black seaweed above the high tide mark to make it pop. The tide was just on the turn, soughing in almost to their feet and then pulling back, the wet seaweed streaming like long hair. *Like a mermaid's hair*, Maureen told her imagination fiercely, refusing to let it develop that other image. *And there lies guid Sir Patrick Spens . . .*

She looked at Shelagh, who was staring down at the water, her hands in the pockets of her cardigan. It was knitted in an Aran pattern of cables, cross-overs and knots. Maureen remembered having read somewhere that in the Western Islands each family had its own pattern. That way, if the body of a drowned fisherman was washed ashore, it could be identified at once by the pattern of the sweater. With the sea today as still as a mill pond, it was difficult to imagine shipwrecks and people drowning.

"The water looks so calm and peaceful, doesn't it?" Shelagh said suddenly.

Maureen looked at her, startled. It was uncanny, as if Shelagh had been reading her mind.

"But d'you know what's out there, between the islands?" Shelagh pointed.

"Between Scarba and Jura, you mean?"

"Yes. Just there. It's a great whirlpool, like the one in *Twenty Thousand Leagues Under the Sea*. Look, at the turn of the tide—like now—you can see the dark line of it from here. It's called the Corrievreken. It can suck a boat right under, did you know that?"

"Shelagh, don't!"

"I can't help it. The sea's so cruel, isn't it? Even when it's beautiful. I keep thinking . . ."

Maureen shivered and turned away from the sea, which had suddenly become unbearable. Looking south she saw something unfamiliar far ahead of them. It was like a tall pillar set in the meadowland above the sea, close under the hill on whose slope Kintray Lodge was built. Thankful for an excuse to change the subject, she interrupted. "What's that over there?"

"Oh, that's just the standing stone." Shelagh's voice sounded indifferent.

"You mean, like the ones at Stonehenge?" Maureen asked excitedly.

"Yes. Except there's only the one here, not a whole ring of them." Shelagh hesitated and her voice suddenly became guarded. "It's not very interesting," she added casually.

"But it must be awfully old. Bronze Age. Maybe even older." Maureen again remembered the head in the burn. Was it all part of the same magic? She was suddenly curious. "Let's walk over and take a look at it." *And get away from the sea*, she thought. *That wasn't a very good idea of Miss Urquhart's, to walk along the shore.*

She clambered eagerly up the rocks onto the spiky grass, where sea pink grew in tufts. She turned. Shelagh was still standing on the shore as if she were reluctant to follow Maureen. "Come on, Shelagh. The shore's so gloomy today. Goodness, this stone may be neolithic, thousands and thousands of years old."

Slowly, reluctantly, Shelagh walked up the slope, scrambled over the pebbly shelf of the raised beach and stood beside her.

"Maybe it's as much as eight thousand years old. Imagine!" Maureen chattered on, relieved to be away from the sea. "I wonder why they put it just here? Do you suppose they worshipped it?"

Shelagh gave a sudden shudder and hugged her chest with her crossed arms. "Och, I don't know. It's just an old stone," she said. But somehow Maureen didn't believe her.

The stone stood like a solitary sentinel upon the highest old beach. It wasn't particularly big. In fact, it wasn't much more than twice Maureen's height, she discovered when they reached it. There was something menacing about it, though, something alien. She rubbed her arms, suddenly feeling prickles of goose-flesh.

I'd hate to be out here at night, she found herself thinking and then told herself not to be silly. It was just the stone's lonely position on the flat shore that made it seem so—so dramatic. She made herself look at it more closely, as if it were an exhibit in a museum. It had been roughly hewn into a four-sided pillar, and she could just detect the remains of carvings upon it, the suggestion of concentric rings, worn by wind and rain to little more than shadows. At its base, though, was something that she would never find in a museum.

"Shelagh, do come and look at this. It's really weird." Maureen knelt at the base of the standing stone, where a little rock shelf had recently been scraped clean of dirt and lichen. Upon it lay a rotting apple and the remains of a sandwich, curling at the edges, that might once have contained fish paste. It looked mummified and slightly disgusting.

"Just the remains of someone's picnic," Shelagh said carelessly. "Nothing odd about it."

"Picnic? But there's no one here on the estate except the school—and the factor. This shore isn't on the way to anywhere. Look, the sandwich hasn't even been touched. Not a bite. And where's the wrapping? There's no grease-proof paper around. And look at the way it's been laid out, so neatly, not as if it's been thrown away. You know what I think, Shelagh? I think it looks more like an offering than someone's leftovers." She straightened up and saw the oddest expression on the other girl's face. Almost like guilt. Shelagh flushed, hesitated and then stammered, "Och, who'd leave an offering *here*? What for?"

Good questions. Why *should* anyone do that? Then something clicked in Maureen's mind: the connection between this strange stone and the carved head in the burn. She remembered the sudden impulse that had made her place a handful of berries on a leaf in front of it. Was this gesture the same? Had someone felt the way *she* had felt?

But it wasn't the same. The stone head had welcomed her, and made her feel good, while this stone . . . She shivered and rubbed her arms again, looking at the worn pillar standing alone on this forlorn shore. "It's uncanny, isn't it? Don't you feel it, Shelagh?"

An artificial smile seemed frozen on Shelagh's face. "It's only a stone," she said again, and Maureen wondered if she were trying to persuade herself.

Shelagh pushed her hands into the pockets of her cardigan and turned away casually—or maybe too casually? At that instant, with a raucous scream, a bird flew suddenly from the bushes behind the standing stone, startling them both.

"Och, that made my heart jump right up," Shelagh said. "But it's only a magpie."

A magpie. *One for sorrow.* Wasn't that what the factor's wife had whispered to Maureen? And here was sorrow, right enough. But that was just a stupid superstition and superstitions were wrong. False idols. Mother would scold her for making such an absurd connection, and she'd be right. After all, this bird could have nothing to do with Shelagh's cousin Geoff. Days and days had probably gone by since the U-boat had slithered into the anchorage at Scapa Flow and sunk *Royal Oak* with its torpedoes. It was the offering in front of the mysterious standing stone, and the memory of the carved head, that had put these strange ideas into her brain.

"The sun's way down in the west," Shelagh said, interrupting her thoughts.

"Time for dinner then. We'd better turn back."

"There's a way up to the house close by here." Shelagh spoke absent-mindedly, but as soon as the words were out she flushed and bit her lip. She'd let something slip, something that Maureen guessed had to be part of the elaborate secret of the Seven Magpies. She pretended not to notice Shelagh's dismay, but started to scramble up the track. It was barely visible, little more than a rabbit's way. Her shoe caught on something. A piece of fine wire.

It wasn't loose, as she discovered when she kicked her foot free, but fastened with twigs in an upright loop. A running noose of fine wire. A snare for rabbits, that's what it was. How horrid! She was tempted to dismantle it and throw it into the bushes, but the factor, MacDougall, would know that one of the academy girls had done it, since there was no once else on the estate. He'd probably complain to Miss Priestley.

She left the snare alone and walked briskly on. The hill rose steeply at first and then began to flatten out. Between the trees Maureen glimpsed the roofs of the lodge. The path divided and Maureen picked the one to the right, the one that seemed to head more directly towards the house.

"Not that way," Shelagh called after her, but Maureen was already well ahead.

"It's bound to finish up at the lodge," she said over her shoulder. "Nowhere else for it to go. Oh, do look!" She stopped suddenly and waited until Shelagh reluctantly caught up with her.

Set into the hillside to their right was a huge wooden door, fastened with an iron bar that nestled in two heavy sockets. Holding the bar to one of the sockets was a large padlock.

"That's really spooky. What do you suppose is behind there?"

Shelagh shrugged and looked evasive. "*I* don't know."

"It's like a dungeon, only who put it there? And why?"

"What a lot of questions you do ask, Maureen Frazer. Come on, or we'll be late for dinner."

Though she didn't really believe it *could* be a dungeon—all the time telling herself what an adventure if it were!—Maureen was quite glad to turn her back on the barred door and run downhill to where the path suddenly ended in the bamboo grove. The lawn beyond the burn still caught a little sunlight, and the sun sparkled off the windows of the lodge. It was all very ordinary and safe. The spookiness she had felt looking at the standing stone and the door in the hillside vanished.

Shelagh caught up with her. "I didn't mean to snap at you, Maureen. Thanks for chumming me. I do feel better."

"Why me, d'you mind my asking? I mean, I'm glad

if I helped a bit. But why not Kathleen or one of your other friends?"

"You're kind. And I just needed to get away."

"What from?"

"Oh, nothing. Don't pay any attention to me. I'm just dithering. We'd better go and wash before dinner." Shelagh ran ahead into the lodge, leaving Maureen with even more unanswered questions.

chapter five

"See if she's asleep, Alison." Kathleen's voice was soft, but loud enough for Maureen, lying in her narrow bed under the window, to hear. She lay still, her eyes closed, willing her breath to come evenly, her eyelids not to flutter, as she felt Alison bend over her bed.

She could feel Alison's breath on her cheek. She kept her eyes tight shut. "It's all right," she heard Alison whisper.

"Then come over here, girls, onto the four-poster. Shove over, Fiona, do."

Maureen could hear faint giggles, rustling and a whispered "shush."

"I don't see why we're meeting here, with *her* in the same room." That was Alison's voice.

"Because this is a special council of war, and it won't wait. First of all, we're all very sorry about your cousin, Shelagh. That's bad luck. But we want to know why you picked *her* instead of one of us to chum you this afternoon."

"Oh, Kathleen!" Peggy exclaimed.

"That's not nice," Moira echoed.

"Shh, girls. I'm not being mean. But it's important that we stick together. That's what belonging to the Magpies is all about, isn't it?"

"Maybe. But when you invented the society, you did say it was for *all* the Lower Fifth, Kath. It doesn't seem fair leaving Maureen out. And she's all right. She's nice."

"Nice or not—and I'd argue with that—she's an outsider, Shelagh. She doesn't count. I don't want her sharing *our* secrets. It could be dangerous."

"But she's already seen the standing stone and the dungeon."

Kathleen sighed impatiently. "And the offering, Shelagh? I suppose she got a peek at that too?"

"Yes, she did. I tried to keep her away, Kathleen, honest, cross my heart. But she was too quick for me. I said it was probably just left by some picnicker, but she knew right off it was an offering."

"You see what I mean, Shelagh?" Kathleen's voice was patient and kind. "If you'd only asked one of us to chum you, this would never have happened."

"I don't care. I'm sick of your old secret society anyway. When we came to Kintray Lodge and you started the Seven Magpies, you said we'd be happy here, that nothing could possibly hurt us. You told us the stone had the power to keep us safe, and as long as we gave it offerings we'd be all right for the Duration. But it isn't true." Maureen heard Shelagh give a muffled sob. "And magpies *are* unlucky. Didn't you know that, Kathleen? We should never have picked them for the name of our secret society."

"Oh, you're just talking nonsense, Shelagh Drummond."

"I am not. Mrs. MacDougall said they were, last time we were down there, remember? 'One for sorrow'. That's the first magpie. And one flew up in front of us, in front of Maureen and me. That proves it."

"Shush, Shelagh. Blow your nose, do. Anyone got a spare handkerchief? If you go on making that noise one of the teachers will hear you. Then they'll be down on us like a ton of bricks. You know Miss Cavanagh prowls at night."

"That's true enough." Maureen recognized Fiona's voice. "She nearly caught me when I was out at the last full moon. I almost died." She giggled. "If I hadn't ducked into the broom cupboard she'd have been onto me."

"Talking of the full moon," Kathleen whispered. "That brings me to the second item of business. Who is to make the next offering to the stone? Tomorrow night is the night of the full moon, remember?"

The silence went on so long that Maureen risked opening her eyes to see what was happening. The moon shone on the four-poster bed. The seven girls huddled on top of the bedspread, not moving. She could see their eyes flash in the moonlight as they looked at one another.

"Come on, girls. When we founded the Secret Society of Magpies, we swore we'd be faithful to the stone if it would protect us. If we miss the full moon offering we break our oath, and who knows what'll happen then. That's how it works."

"Well, I went last month, so I'm off the hook, thank goodness," Fiona whispered cheerfully. "I tell you, it was really creepy. You have no idea what it's like out there at night, especially going past the dungeon, expecting something to jump out at you any minute. I wouldn't do it again for all the tea in China." Maureen saw her shiver dramatically.

There was another long silence. "How about *you* going, Kath?" That was Eileen's voice.

"You know very well I founded the society, and the first rule is that every new member has to make the offering—one member each full moon. But I don't have to initiate myself into my own society. That's dumb."

"It's not very fair," Shelagh put in. "And I'm not going, so there. I don't believe that the stone *is* magic. Not anymore. Not after what happened to Geoff."

"Look, perhaps we *should* invite her to be a member," Alison said quickly. "It'd be a lot safer with her as one of us, don't you think, Kathleen?"

"You've got a point there. She wouldn't be able to

tell on us then, not after swearing the oath," Eileen added.

"She wouldn't tell anyway," Shelagh argued. "I heard her talking to Miss Cavanagh just outside the door the night of the last full moon. She let Miss C. think that she was the one who'd been prowling, and she didn't have to do that. And she didn't pry and ask what Fiona'd been doing afterwards. You were awake that night, Kathleen, waiting for Fiona to come back safely. You must have heard Maureen too. You know she wouldn't tell on us. So how come you're so against her?"

There was a long pause. Maureen could feel Kathleen's anger and the tension in the other six, as they waited to see if that anger would explode.

Why do they put up with her bossiness? she wondered again. But then, as she thought about Kathleen's invention of the secret society, she realized what a clever idea it had been. And not all bad. It had bound them together into a comfortable group when they were in a strange place, far from their families, afraid of what being at war might mean.

She remembered that first Sunday, the third of September, and how terrified *she* had been when the sirens had begun to wail. She had felt the panic rising inside her as they had looked east to see if enemy airplanes were coming. Then Daddy had put his arm across her shoulder and everything had been all right again.

I would probably have joined the Magpies myself back then, she owned to herself.

"Well?" Shelagh broke the long silence.

"I'm not actually *against* her, Shelagh." Kathleen's voice was conciliatory. "Not really. But she's a bit of a swot and she's not one of us, is she? But if you think she should come in, we'll vote on it right now. Who's for admitting her? Put your hands up. Shelagh. Alison. Eileen. That's three for. Moira, Fiona and Peggy against. So it's up to me to decide."

"What I was thinking, Kathleen, was that *she* could make the next offering. That's why I suggested we should invite her to join."

Maureen saw the figures on the bed suddenly relax, look at each other.

"That's brilliant, Alison. All right. What do you others think of that idea? Fiona? Peggy? Moira? Do you want to change your vote? All right, girls. She's in. We'll tell her what she has to do after school tomorrow."

"But shouldn't we tell her sooner? The offering . . ." Shelagh began.

"No. *After* school. Meeting adjourned."

Maureen closed her eyes as the other girls went back to their own beds. Just before she fell asleep she thought: *I still don't know what Kathleen thinks about letting me belong. She never did vote.*

* * *

In the free time before dinner and the second study period, Kathleen nodded meaningfully to the six and

said to Maureen, "Come on down to the bamboo
grove. We want to talk to you."

Maureen was tempted to tell her to go jump in the
loch, but she *was* curious to find out more about the
Magpies than she already knew. Trying to hide her
interest she said, "Oh, all right," and slowly put her
books away in her desk.

The Lower Fourth were playing some elaborate war
game in the grove when the Lower Fifth arrived.
"Out," said Kathleen imperiously.

"But we were here first. It's not fair."

"Doesn't matter. It's Lower Fifth's special place and
don't you forget it. Now off with you."

Originally the grove had been planted in a circle,
but the bamboo stems had multiplied until now there
was barely room to squeeze into the open space in the
centre. Inside, it was like being in a secret room, with
walls hung with tattered silk. The breeze whispered in
the leaves, but the centre was still and quiet.

"Be careful where you sit," Peggy warned Maureen
as they settled down. "There's a bamboo torture where
they peg you onto the ground and let the bamboo
shoots grow right through your body."

"Peggy, you're making that up." Moira shuddered.

"I am not. I read it in a book."

"Come to order," Kathleen said solemnly. "Maureen Frazer, you have been admitted to our special
meeting place so that we can invite you to become a
member of the Secret Society of Magpies."

It was funny. Only a month ago, Maureen realized,

she would have been ecstatic at such an offer. To become part of the group! Now it didn't matter in the same way. She had made some mysterious contact with the land through her offering to the stone head and had found a kind of belonging.

"Thank you," she said formally. "Could you tell me a bit more about the society before I decide?"

"Before *you* decide!" Kathleen spluttered. Maureen saw the others look meaningfully at their leader. She swallowed, attempted a smile and went on. "I suppose that's all right. But you must promise never to tell anyone else. Do you promise?"

"Aye, I do."

"Well, then. As you know, Logan Academy was evacuated from Saint Andrews at the beginning of September, the day after war was declared. It was a rough experience, being separated so suddenly from our families. We needed something to bring us together, to make us a kind of unit. A society. 'One for all and all for one', you know."

Maureen nodded. "Of course. Only 'Magpies' instead of 'Musketeers'."

"Er . . . yes." Kathleen seemed taken aback by Maureen's interruption. *She's probably never even read* The Three Musketeers, Maureen thought to herself.

"Who picked you as leader, Kathleen?" she asked abruptly. The others looked at her blankly and then turned their heads towards Kathleen. "I suppose you all voted for her?" she added innocently.

Kathleen's face turned fiery red. "The society was

my idea. And we don't *have* to invite you in, you know. You've got an awful nerve, asking all these questions, and you just a new girl."

"But we *did* vote to invite Maureen in," Shelagh said. "We agreed."

"You six did. I didn't cast a vote."

"But . . ."

Maureen unfolded her legs and stood up. "Maybe I'd better leave while you work this out."

"But we've *told* you. You've got to be in. You've got to take the oath of secrecy so you won't blab to the teachers."

"I didn't blab about Fiona being out at night a month ago. What *were* you doing, Fiona? Putting an offering under the standing stone?"

"Shelagh, you *did* tell!"

"No, I didn't, honest. I told you, she's smart. She worked it out for herself."

Maureen nodded. "It was kind of obvious. There's bits about offerings in one of the library books on Celtic history I was reading. I suppose you decided that the standing stone was magic and that it would keep you safe from the war. Actually, I think you're dead wrong. I don't think it works that way—not with the stone. There was nothing in the book about offerings to standing stones. And . . ." She hesitated. "If it *were* magic, I don't think it would necessarily be *good* magic."

"Och, what do *you* know!" Fiona exploded.

Maureen hesitated. Maybe she should tell them of her strong feeling that the standing stone was dark magic. But she couldn't really explain why without bringing in the stone head, and she didn't want to do that. They'd only laugh at her anyway. She shrugged. "What do I know? Nothing, probably. I just mentioned it. But anyway, you don't have to worry. I won't tell on you."

She pushed her way out of the grove and walked down to the burn. With so little rain this autumn it was in danger of drying up. There'd be more bath rationing soon, if the trickle here was any indication of the amount of water up on the moor. She was just thinking how much nicer it would be if it were summer, and they could go swimming instead of having only a weekly bath in a miserable five inches of water, when Kathleen called her back.

"We've decided to accept you into the Magpies," Kathleen said. "And you've been chosen to make the next offering to the stone. Congratulations."

She didn't look very pleased while she said this. Maureen wondered if they'd ever be friends. Suddenly she found she could see the situation from Kathleen's point of view. Maureen had arrived late at school, she had the wrong uniform and she was better than Kathleen at maths *and* English. That was quite enough to make Kathleen dislike her. But there was more to it than that.

It was as if the Lower Fifth had grown together into a unit like a wall, a dry wall made of different stones closely packed together, secure against outside pressures. Just like the stone fences all over Scotland.

Then along came Maureen Frazer, like an extra stone. How were they going to fit her in? Did they want to? And why should they?

She *did* have choices. She could shape herself into their image, a young lady belonging to Logan Academy, and fit herself in. Or she could force herself, just as she was, with all her own awkward corners, in among the other stones, even if she spoiled the look of the wall. Or she could stay outside and not be part of the wall at all.

But being alone outside the "wall" for the Duration was almost too miserable to think of. She'd had to endure it for over a month. Could she stand it anymore? Maybe it would be all right to go along with their ideas. Maybe she should agree to take their silly offering to the standing stone, even if she didn't believe it was a wise thing to do.

Well, what was the worst that could happen to her? One of the teachers might catch her and she'd be expelled. *That* wouldn't be much of a loss. Mother would have to let her go back to her old school in Saint Andrews or send her to stay with Gran in Edinburgh. Either choice would be wonderful.

She nodded. "All right. I'll do it."

The others visibly relaxed. Kathleen nodded. "Good. Now, first of all, you've got to take a solemn oath never to divulge to a living soul the secrets of the Magpies. Do you so swear?"

"I'll not swear. Swearing's against the Commandments. But I'll give you my word."

Kathleen frowned. "The others all swore the oath."

There I go again, thought Maureen. *Forcing in my stone instead of shaping it the way they want.*

"Her word should do, Kath. She never told on me," Fiona said, and the others nodded.

"All right. But I hope you won't all live to regret it, girls. The full moon's tonight, Maureen, so be prepared."

"Prepared?"

"What you have to do is take fruit and meat to the stone. That's the proper offering, or else the magic won't work."

"Where am I going to get the fruit and meat from?"

"You'll have to sneak them out of the dining room without anyone else seeing, especially the teachers."

"But why didn't you tell me before lunch?" She stared at Kathleen. So that's what Shelagh had been objecting to in the whispered conference last night! It really wasn't fair. The last month's offering of a fish paste sandwich and apple had obviously come from lunch, always a free and easy meal of fruit and sandwiches. All Fiona had had to do was help herself to extras and tuck them in her pocket, with no one the wiser. Dinner was different. Dinner was a formal meal, and the teachers' eyes were always on them, checking for good manners.

"Of course, you can always change your mind," Kathleen suggested, smirking triumphantly.

"Certainly not." Maureen stuck her chin out. "I'll do it. You don't have to worry."

"Oh, *I'm* not worried. But *you'd* better look out. Remember, Miss Priestley's got eyes in the back of her head."

The only preparation that Maureen could think to make was to tuck a clean handkerchief in her pocket; as soon as she sat down for dinner and spread her napkin in her lap, she smoothed the handkerchief over it and waited for the plates to be passed. Everything now depended on what was being served. Roast lamb or stewed rabbit would be just fine. Or meatloaf would do. She'd put a helping on her plate and smuggle a tiny portion into the handkerchief on her lap.

The plates were passed down the table and her heart sank. *Mince*—with mashed potatoes and mashed turnips. Her least favourite meal in the world. But even worse, it was far too messy to smuggle out of the dining room in a handkerchief. The ground meat swimming in salted gravy was almost too sloppy to eat with a fork. Only by mashing the mince in with the potatoes could the girls manage.

Maureen looked up from her plate in time to see Kathleen flash a triumphant grin at the others. She looked down at her plate again and went on scooping up the disagreeable mess. *I bet she knew what was for dinner all the time*, she thought. When dessert arrived— Sally-before-the-bath—Maureen was almost sure of it.

An offering of meat and fruit—and she had neither so far. Well, if this was to be a test of her ingenuity, she'd find a way. She gritted her teeth and outstared Kathleen.

On the day the Lower Fifth had picked blaeberries for tarts, Maureen had seen the layout of the kitchen. She knew that perishables were kept in a cool stone larder facing north, while root vegetables, apples and dry goods like sugar, flour and oatmeal were stored in a large walk-in pantry off the kitchen. Now that Miss Priestly had hired a regular kitchen staff, the whole kitchen area was out of bounds to students. As soon as dinner was over Maureen drifted over to the serving hatch and had a quick look around. It was hopeless. The pantry door was locked. The larder would be impossible to reach, unless . . .

"Yes? Were you wanting something?" It was the cook, hands on hips, guarding her territory.

"N-no, thank you."

"If you was cadging seconds or sneaking a look at my larder, you can forget it. There's a shortage of food, I'll remind you, young lady, and fair's fair."

"Of course. I didn't mean to . . ." Seeing Miss Priestley's eyes on her, Maureen bolted for the door.

"What are you going to do?" Shelagh whispered on their way out of the dining room.

"Oh, I'll think of something," Maureen replied lightly, though her mind was a blank. She told herself that it didn't matter. It was only a stupid game, after all. But during the supervised study after dinner, she found herself staring at Caesar's *Gallic Wars* without being able to construe a single sentence of his Latin into acceptable English.

After study there was recreation, and the whole

school gathered around the piano in what had once been the ballroom and was now the assembly hall. It had a real stage at one end, perfect for plays, where the band would have been set up for dances in the old days. One of the senior girls dashed off the latest songs and everyone joined in singing the words.

> Run, rabbit, run, rabbit, run, run, run.
> Don't give the farmer his fun, fun, fun.
> He'll get by without his apple pie.
> So run rabbit, run rabbit, run.

It was while they were singing this particular ditty that Maureen had her inspiration. It was horrible, but if she could bring herself to do it and if she were lucky, half her problem would be solved.

As for the second half, Fiona came over to where she stood on the edge of the crowd and said quietly, "I had to take some books into the staff common room for Miss Cavanagh. There's a bowl of apples on the table."

Maureen managed a smile. "Thanks."

"Och, not at all. And you know you'll have to get out of a window? The front door is locked and bolted and that's the first place the teachers check on their rounds."

Maureen hadn't known about the door being bolted. Typical of Kathleen not to mention it. *She wants to get me expelled*, she suddenly realized, *so everything can go on the way it did before I got here.*

Well, I won't get caught, so you can swallow that, Kathleen Buchanan!

At bedtime she put on her nightie over her underwear and then lay under the bedclothes, waiting for the moon to appear. Her heart was pounding and there was a fluttery feeling in her stomach, but at the same time she was excited. *And Fiona managed, so surely I can.*

When the first sliver of moonlight appeared she got quietly out of bed. She could tell that the others were awake. She could feel their eyes on her, though nobody said a word. She put on a cardigan over her nightie, tucked her little torch safely in one of the pockets and took her gym shoes in her hand. It would be difficult to explain these if she were caught, but there was no way she was going down that steep track to the shore in bedroom slippers. If she were caught, maybe she could pretend to be sleepwalking.

She eased the door open and slid out into the corridor. It was dark except for a thin line of white where the moon came in through a window above the stairs. She stood perfectly still, ready to duck back into the dorm if necessary, trying to breathe slowly and quietly while she listened. Two floors down the grandfather clock in the hall tick-tocked. There was no other sound, nothing to mask the tiny creak of her feet on the stairs—which would surely sound as loud as a cannon to anyone lying awake, listening.

A sudden whirring made her jump. Then she realized that the sound was the perfect cover. She ran barefoot down the two flights of stairs, not pausing until she had found a patch of deep shadow in the main hall. The clock had just finished the full four Westminster chimes and was striking the hour when she reached her goal. She stood very still, waiting for it to finish . . . ten . . . eleven . . . twelve. She strained her ears past its deep, regular tick-tock. There was no other sound.

She slid past Miss Priestley's study to the door of the staff common room. She had never been inside. If a teacher were needed, one knocked, waited for the door to open and gave one's message. Now the door-knob slipped under Maureen's sweaty hand and wouldn't turn. She wiped her palm on her cardigan and tried again. The door swung open.

Unspoiled by school furniture, it was a pretty room, even with the colours of the chintz-covered easy chairs bleached to black, grey and white in the moonlight shining through the leaded windows. On a small table with curved legs in the centre were a copy of *The Scotsman* and a bowl with three apples in it. When she had taken one and dropped it safely into her cardigan pocket the remaining two looked very lonely. She hoped no one had counted them, but there was no point worrying about that. She still had to get out of the lodge without being detected.

Unlike the heavy sash windows upstairs, the windows in this part of the building were casements with simple latches. She pushed the latch down, opened the window and climbed through. For a moment she got stuck and almost panicked, but it was only her cardigan catching on the frame. She wriggled through and dropped to the rose bed outside. She pushed the window almost closed, leaving just enough finger room to pull it open again. Then she squatted behind the roses, the prickles catching at her hair and cardigan, and struggled into her gym shoes.

The sweep of gravel driveway in front of the lodge was bathed in moonlight. It was like a moat around a castle, guarding the sleeping inhabitants from intruders. She was going to have to cross it, noisy and very visible; there was no way of being subtle about it. Taking a deep breath she leapt across, hearing the scutter of stones against the rubber soles of her shoes, and then hurtled down the far slope. She crossed the burn in a single leap and ducked into the shadow of the bamboo grove.

As she caught her breath and tried to slow her thumping heart, she glanced back at the lodge. How grand it looked on its hill, silhouetted against the dark sky behind. It seemed quiet. No alarm had been raised. Or was that the gleam of a torch on the second floor? Perhaps it was just the moon reflected on a window. She told herself that it was useless to worry about that now. The worst of her adventure was still ahead of her.

When they had been singing "Run, Rabbit, Run" she had remembered the rabbit snare she had seen the day before, set on the sandy hill among the bushes and scrub. That was the way she must go now. It was very dark among the trees. She held her torch in the palm of her hand so that only the faintest gleam of light escaped between her fingers, just enough to show her the small sandy tracks of a rabbit runway. She walked along tracing the track, bent over close to the ground. Her torch found a snare, but it was empty.

Suppose they were all empty? If the factor had come along in the evening to see what he had caught, then her bright idea would be useless. It might be even worse if she were to find a snare with a live rabbit in it. What would she do then? She couldn't possibly kill it.

She swallowed, took a steadying breath and walked on. What a long time she was taking! She straightened up and saw that the moon had already moved across the southern sky and was standing high over the sea.

Then she saw the rabbit, lying stretched to its full length, as if it had gone on running and running desperately in place until the noose had finally, mercifully, choked it to death. She laid the torch down and knelt on the sandy ground. Its fur was so soft, beigy-brown on top and white underneath. It was limp, not stiff, so it couldn't have died long ago. Shuddering, she dug her fingers into the fur of its neck until they felt the cruel wire noose and she loosened it and slipped it over the rabbit's head and ears. The teeth gleamed in a grimace and the eyes were open and bulging. They were nothing like the eyes of a live animal, but more like the glazed and empty ones of the rabbits in the butcher's shop back in Saint Andrews, hanging by their feet. For sale.

She told herself firmly that the poor little rabbit was dead already, as dead as the ones in the butcher's shop. She remembered to straighten out the wire, to place it in its circle of twigs and to smooth away her handprints from the sandy soil. It would never do for the factor to start asking questions about who had been at his traps.

Her heart was thumping and she felt a little sick as she picked up the rabbit by its hind legs and began to scramble down the steep path that led to the standing stone. Concentrating on not tripping over a rock or a protruding root, she came out unexpectedly at the edge of the trees to see the stone outlined against the sea, dead ahead of her.

She was so startled that she stopped abruptly. The moon hung in the southwestern sky, flooding the ancient grass-covered beach and the loch beyond with a light as strong as a floodlight. Its brilliance dimmed the starlight so that there seemed to be nothing up there but the white circle, stamped out of a sheet of silver, hanging like a locket above a fantastic landscape of black and white. The standing stone was like a great finger pointing up towards it. Ancient. Menacing.

Maureen shivered. It was almost as if the moon were pouring out cold rays, the way the sun poured out warmth. Evil instead of good. She told herself not to be fanciful and quickly crossed the last few yards until she was standing directly beneath the stone. She crouched beside the flat rock at its base. The withered apple and the disgusting remains of mouldy sandwich were still there, and she found a flat piece of stone to scrape them off into the grass. Then she laid the rabbit on its side, stretched out, and placed the apple between the forepaws. She wasn't quite sure why she did this, but it felt right.

Then she got slowly to her feet, hugging her arms across her chest, and looked up at the standing stone. It had a very different *feel* from the head in the burn. That ancient stone was also uncanny but, in a strange way, friendly. She had felt as if she had done something right and proper when she had left her offering there.

This stone was different. From a different time, made for a different reason. What she had just done made her feel at odds with herself, uncomfortable. If there were any power here, it was not for good.

She shuddered and set off quickly up the track towards the lodge. In the shadow of the hill it was dark again, and she had to use her torch to make sure she stayed on the path. It branched and she hesitated. They'd gone to the right last time, she remembered, she and Shelagh. She went that way again and had walked fifty yards or so up the path before she remembered the door into the hill.

I wish I'd gone the other way, she thought, and almost turned back. *Don't be silly. It's just a door, barred and padlocked. That's all.* But the closer she got to it, the harder it was *not* to picture the door swinging open and something coming out after her. Or, even worse, the door swinging open and *nothing* coming out. Just a terrible black emptiness.

Her torch bulb was little more than a firefly light as she hurried by, refusing to look to the right, but not being able to stop herself from imagining that, at any minute, something might reach out and grab her. By the time she had scrambled to the top of the hill, to see the lodge sprawled out below her, she could hardly breathe. Fear clamped around her ribs like steel fingers. She stopped and forced a shaky breath into her lungs, then let it out slowly, telling herself that everything was all right. She had done it. It was over.

The moon shone on the west side of the lodge now, making the turrets look even more magical than they looked by day. The driveway was still illuminated as unforgivingly as before, but the rose bed under the staff room window was in deep, welcoming shadow.

Almost home free.

She ran lightly across the gravel and crouched under the sill, tugging at the window with her fingertips. How stiff it was. Suppose she couldn't get it open? What would she do? *Come on, now! Open!* She felt a fingernail break at the same instant that the window finally budged. She dragged it open, pulled herself up onto the sill and remembered, just in time, to slip off her soiled gym shoes before swinging her legs over and dropping down onto the carpet on the inside.

Two minutes later she had retraced her steps upstairs and was safely in bed, shivering under her blankets. The hem of her nightie was wet with dew, and her hands and feet were blocks of ice. When she rubbed her hands together and held them close to her body for warmth, she could smell the wild animal smell of the rabbit. She squeezed her eyes shut and lay rigid, longing for sleep, while the moon finished its journey around the dorm and finally left the room in darkness.

CHAPTER SIX

"I just don't believe you did it. You wouldn't have had the nerve!"

"I did, too, Kathleen Buchanan. You're just trying to get out of having me in the Magpies. Well, I don't care, so there!" Maureen slammed out of the dorm, bumping into Miss Cavanagh in the passage outside.

"Gently, Maureen, please. Remember that you are a young lady, not a hooligan."

It was the start of a miserable day. There was no letter from Daddy, and the one from Mother was almost a carbon copy of the ones Maureen had already received.

> London full of interesting people. Almost worn out dining and dancing, but that is part of war work too, isn't it?

Who was taking her? People didn't go dining and dancing by themselves, after all. Was it the same man she'd written about in an earlier letter? What about Daddy? She never said how much she missed *him*; she didn't even mention him in her letter, not once.

At least nothing much was going on in Europe. All the news that filtered down to the students had to do with the *Graf Spee* sinking a liner off the coast of South America and then hiding so the British battle-ships couldn't get at it. Sometimes the war seemed a very long way off and unreal. In spite of the sinking of *Royal Oak*, the Nazis weren't invading Scotland, so why was she stuck in this school in the middle of nowhere?

"Maureen, what *are* you dreaming about? I've called your name twice. Please construe the next passage."

She got to her feet and stumbled through *Caesar*. This particular passage said that the Germani were covered with hair. Who cared? Those wars had all happened such a very long time ago and had been quite different from *this* war. There had been no U-boats then, no sunken destroyers or battleships. The Germani weren't even related to present-day Germans, but were more like the Celts.

Fiona, who was often silly about such things, got the giggles at the idea of the hairy Germani and was sent out of class.

Maureen sat down again thankfully and lapsed into a dream in which she was back in Saint Andrews, going on a picnic with Daddy, just the two of them walking in the hills, with hard-boiled eggs and ham sandwiches for their lunch. Vaguely, like an annoying background sound, she could hear the faint whisper of Shelagh arguing with Kathleen and Alison.

"Be quiet, please." Miss Urquhart rapped the desk. "I don't know what's got into you all today, but I'll remind you that it won't be that many months till exam time, so pull yourselves together."

Maureen stifled a yawn that made her jaws crack and her eyes water. And now Kathleen didn't believe her. What a waste of a good night's sleep. *I'll get a nap before dinner*, she promised herself, and tried pinching her arms to stay awake.

Kathleen caught her after study period. "We've decided that the fair thing would be for us to go down to the stone and see this offering you say you put there."

"You go if you want, Kathleen. I just don't care. If you don't believe me, that's your lookout, not mine." She yawned again and went upstairs to get a cardigan. She couldn't risk napping in the dorm. One of the teachers would be sure to notice and ask her if she were ill. But she had found a quiet spot in the pine woods, sheltered from the wind, where no one would bother her. It was quite her favourite place when she felt she had to get away from everybody.

She lay on the soft pine needles and looked up through the straight slender trees. They all seemed to crowd together at their tips, like long bony fingers pointing towards the circle of sky just above her head.

As they swayed gently to and fro, the soughing of the wind muffled the other sudden sounds of girls laughing, calling to each other, the rhythmic *tock* of a tennis ball against a racquet. Beneath her spine she could feel the earth and imagined the whole planet spinning around the sun, taking her with it. The forest smelled bitter, autumnal. Her eyes closed and she slept.

* * *

"There she is!"

Maureen sat up with a jolt, shedding needles from her hair. She brushed them from her cardigan and shivered. How long had she been asleep?

"Well, what a fibber!" exclaimed Kathleen.

"I always knew you would shirk it," added Peggy, and Moira chimed in, "What a stupid story. As if we'd believe *that*."

They stood over her, hands on hips, all alike in their green skirts and cardigans, while she sat there, still half asleep, the alien one. They had wakened her from a wonderful dream. She and Daddy and Mother had been tramping through the woods, dodging among the trees, laughing together. But now it was gone. A silly dream, really. Mother had never enjoyed going for hikes. She was a town person, not like Daddy.

Maureen got slowly to her feet and began to brush the needles off her uniform. She felt cold and sad and completely alone. "I don't know what you're talking about," she muttered.

"We went down to the stone and there's no offering there at all."

She stared. "What are you on about? There must be. I told you I put them there. A rabbit and an apple."

"They're not there now. So how're you going to prove you did it?"

"You'll just have to go again tonight," Kathleen said firmly.

"I will not. It's not fair. I did it."

"Then where's the offering?"

"Och, you're just putting me on." Maureen pushed out of the circle and ran down the slope towards the lodge. As she reached the burn, curiosity overcame her and impulsively she turned along it, past the bamboo grove, scrambling over the sandy flank of the hill and down to the beach meadow. It was funny. Last night the journey had seemed impossibly long, but in daylight it took almost no time at all. Before she knew it she was standing beneath the stone itself, staring at the flat rock at its base.

No rabbit. No apple.

"But I *did*," she said out loud. She could still remember the feel of soft fur, the glazed look of the bloodshot eyes, the grimacing teeth. She shivered and wrapped her arms around her body. Then she walked back to the lodge for dinner.

Nobody spoke to her at the table or afterwards, not even when they got ready for bed. They talked as if she weren't there.

"Maybe she's telling the truth," Fiona said, hesitatingly.

"Did you see her expression when we told her we'd been down to the stone? Guilty," Alison retorted.

"I thought she just looked surprised," Shelagh argued.

"Surprised? She was putting it on," Kathleen said. "If she isn't lying, then where's the rabbit?"

"Maybe it wasn't dead. Maybe it ran away," Shelagh suggested.

"Could it have run away, Maureen?"

She turned on them. "Och, you're all so stupid. Of course it was dead. Very, very dead. I had an awful time getting the wire off its neck. Then I carried it down to the stone and put it on that piece of rock with the apple between its front paws. If I'm not lying, then maybe the apple ran away too. Why don't you ask the *real* question? If I'm telling the truth—and I am—then who took the offering away?"

She picked up her sponge bag and towel and went off to the bathroom, leaving them staring at each other. When she got back she knew something had changed. She felt that more of them were on her side, maybe all except Alison and Kathleen. Feeling just as uncomfortable as before, she got into bed, shut her eyes and said her prayers.

Kathleen must have been doing a lot of thinking that night too, because in the morning, while they were making their beds, she said, "Maureen, I am willing for you to stay a member of the Magpies."

The others stared. "So what turned you round? You don't really believe *her* story, do you?" Moira and Peggy exclaimed together.

Kathleen nodded solemnly. She looked directly at each of them in turn. Maureen could feel her willing them to believe her—the same way, probably, that she'd made them believe the whole strange story of the power of the Magpies and the standing stone. "We always knew the stone was magical, didn't we? That's why we began making offerings in the first place. Well, the stone has accepted Maureen's offering. That's why it's gone. It's a sign!"

"Och, that's weird." Shelagh hugged her pillow and shivered.

"It's ridiculous," said Eileen rudely, suddenly losing her Logan Academy accent. "Where would it go?"

"Into the spirit world, of course." Kathleen rolled her r's and managed to sound impressively spooky. The others looked at each other.

Moira broke the silence. "But it's only a kind of *game*, isn't it? I mean, we don't really *believe* in the standing stone and the Magpies and all that . . ." Her voice trailed off into silence as Kathleen stared coldly at her.

"You swore an oath, Moira. All of you did." Her eyes swept over the group. "Why did you swear, if you didn't believe?"

There was another silence.

"But if it *is* really magic, why didn't the stone take *my* offering?" Fiona objected.

"It probably didn't like the fish paste," Eileen put in dryly, and the tension broke.

The others began to laugh. "I don't blame it."

"Ugh, fish paste!"

Maureen smoothed her bedspread, keeping an eye on Kathleen. She wouldn't like this laughter, she guessed. It drowned out the eerie feeling she was trying to create.

"Don't laugh," Kathleen warned, her voice dramatically deep, "or you'll be sorry. If you offend the spirit of the stone something awful is bound to happen. The stone wanted a *blood* sacrifice. That's why it rejected the other offering, don't you see? And we all know what happened then."

"What?"

"It was after Fiona's offering that Shelagh's cousin was lost on *Royal Oak*."

"That's a terrible thing to say, Kathleen." Maureen jumped to her feet. "It's wicked. Geoff's death has nothing to do with the stone. It *couldn't*."

"How do you know, smartie? People keep four-leaf clovers, don't they? And rabbits' feet? All sorts of lucky charms. They must work, or people wouldn't bother." She looked triumphantly at each of them in turn.

"But—" Peggy began and then stopped.

"And the stone is *far* more powerful than a sprig of clover. You can tell, can't you? And it's on our side now."

"I don't know," Moira began to object.

"And there's the Magpies," Kathleen went on quickly. "It's all coming true, the way I knew it would.

The first magpie is for sorrow. We all know about that one—Shelagh's cousin. The second is for joy. That's the stone accepting our sacrifice."

"What about the third, then? 'Three for a girl', isn't it?"

"That's Maureen. She's the strange girl coming into our midst. That's why we have to accept her into the Magpies."

Maureen shook her head. Kathleen's argument couldn't possibly be true. Yet, in a muddled sort of way, it made sense. The others were certainly impressed by it; she could tell by their faces. Their attitude towards Maureen had been like a scale, weight balancing against weight. Sometimes they were on her side. Sometimes they weren't. But their changes hadn't made a blind bit of difference because Kathleen had always been against her, weighing the other side of the scale down. Now Kathleen had shifted, and she was pulling the others with her. Maureen was *in*—but for all the wrong reasons. Not because Kathleen wanted her to belong, but because that was the only way Kathleen could keep her power over the others, by making them believe in the stone.

I should be pleased. But I'm not. Blood sacrifice. That's nasty. And a thought flashed through her mind: *Kathleen's going to want to repeat it the next time the moon is full.*

I won't have anything to do with it if she does, Maureen told herself firmly. *It's all wicked superstition.* Then she found herself remembering the stone head in the burn, with its bulging eyes. Like the rabbit's?

No, not a bit. The eyes of the carved head were blind but all-seeing, as the book had said. And that's why she'd given it the berries.

Not a *fear* sacrifice, but a *gift*. Like dropping a penny in the Forth when you crossed the great bridge over the river. *Out of a kind of respect*, she told herself. *That's what makes the difference.*

* * *

The next Saturday Miss Priestley sent them up onto the moor to cut sphagnum moss for the war effort. They filled bags with the stuff, bulky but feather light. "It'll be used to make dressings for the wounded," Miss Priestley told them.

"What wounded?" they'd all asked. In this magically soft, sunny place, so different from Saint Andrews with its bracing climate, it was increasingly hard to believe in the war. And there was still very little in the news.

"There'll be wounded enough before we're through, I'm afraid," Miss Priestley said in answer to their questions. "And sphagnum moss has natural antiseptic qualities that will help heal our brave soldiers."

Maureen thought of Daddy standing guard somewhere in France, and shivered. The grown-ups had said that the Maginot Line was impregnable and that the Nazis could never invade France. But . . .

"It's all right," Kathleen whispered to her. "Nothing bad will happen. You're a Magpie now." And, though the idea was quite ridiculous and she told herself firmly that she didn't believe it, Kathleen's soothing words suddenly made her feel better.

After they'd filled all the sacks with moss, Miss Priestley gave them a surprise picnic. It was a real celebration, with sardine sandwiches, potato salad and hard-boiled eggs. They were lucky that Mrs. MacDougall kept hens. Eggs were already in short supply as they'd heard in letters from home. Afterwards, there were squares of dark treacly gingerbread, deliciously spicy and filling.

When she had finished eating, Maureen slipped away from the others. She told herself that she just wanted to be alone for a while, and that it was only chance that drew her in a southeasterly direction across the moor. She walked slowly down the slope towards the glen, knowing that eventually she must come to the burn that drained the bog.

Once she came upon the burn, she found herself walking slowly uphill again, as she had done before. This time she almost missed the stone head. Well, she hadn't really been looking for it. Or had she?

It was just as she had remembered it, almost hidden under the overhanging grass. She sat down beside the water, looking southwards, following the gaze of the ancient eyes. She noticed that they had no pupils, like the eyes of statues carved later by the Greeks and Romans. Perhaps the carvers didn't know how to add the pupils, or perhaps they left the eyes blind deliberately. The book in the library had said that the stone heads could "see" in a different kind of way. They could see into the past. Or into the future.

The future? She decided she wouldn't want to know about that. There were too many scary possibilities. With her hands linked around her knees, Maureen sat and began to imagine what the landscape might have been like thousands of years ago, when this stone head had first looked south across this particular valley.

There'd have been trees, of course, far more than there were now. And not orderly plantations of larch and pine either, but a wild and variegated forest, alive with great stags and wild boars. She imagined a boar, with flaming red eyes and shining tusks, charging up the hill towards her. It was almost real. So real that, when she saw the bracken down in the valley quiver, she found herself on her feet, staring down, her heart pounding like mad.

What a dummy, she told herself, wiping her suddenly damp hands on the sides of her gym tunic. *There's nothing down there but an old rabbit.*

From the advantage of her position, halfway up the steep slope, she could see a stealthy movement eastwards through the bracken, away from the loch and towards the hill. Then she blinked, rubbed her eyes and stared again. Was she seeing things? A rabbit didn't have red hair, or an old tweed jacket. By the time she focused again on the spot where she had last seen him, whoever it was had vanished among the trees—as if he had never been. Maybe he had been her imagination after all, like the wild boar.

Hair reddish-gold, like the bracken. A tweed jacket, brown like the bracken. "Maybe it *was* just bracken?" Maureen wondered aloud. She turned and looked at the stone head in the burn. Its blank, bulging eyes stared down the hillside. "Did *you* see him?"

The mouth curved in its secret smile. The only sound was the ripple of the burn around the square carved stone. She hesitated. "There aren't any more blaeberries," she said aloud. "I've got nothing." Her hands dug automatically into her blazer pockets. One grubby cotton handkerchief. A half-sucked sweetie covered with fluff from her pocket. And a threepenny piece.

Something after all. When she dropped the coin into the water in front of the carved stone, the profile of the young king's head uppermost, the water rippled over it, making it seem mint-new, larger than life. It looked lovely shining there. She turned away feeling, for the moment, at peace with the world.

As she climbed up to the top of the moor to join the others she wondered again what she had seen. Was it a crouching man? If so where could he have come from? There was nothing to the west but the rocky shoreline. Beyond it, the islands. Ireland a bit to the south. And the Atlantic Ocean, where enemy submarines lurked.

Perhaps there was a perfectly innocent explanation. Maybe he was the factor of a nearby estate. Only why had he been crawling through the bracken on hands and knees like a fugitive? Or a *spy*?

"Where *have* you been?" Kathleen said crossly, as Maureen came in sight of the others. "I wish you wouldn't wander off in that odd way. Miss Priestley wants us to carry the sacks of moss down to the lodge."

"I was walking over there," Maureen pointed vaguely. "I think I saw someone. Who could it have been? A spy, do you think? Maybe I should tell Miss Priestley."

"Hush." Kathleen's eyes gleamed with excitement. "Don't say a word."

"Why on earth not?"

"This is a matter for the Magpies. Let's take these old sacks down and then we'll all meet in the bamboo grove. Come on. Don't dawdle," she added bossily and ran off to tell the others.

"Goodness, you sound just like my mother," Maureen grumbled, as she hauled her sack down the hill.

But later, sitting with the seven in the secrecy of the bamboo grove, she felt pleasantly important telling them exactly what she'd seen, leaving out her private imaginings about the prehistoric boar, of course. "And I sort of wondered . . . do you suppose he was a *spy*?"

"How'd he get here?" Alison asked practically. "And what on earth is there to spy on?"

They stared blankly at each other, until Kathleen said quickly, "Off a U-boat. We all know they're lurking out there underwater in the Irish Sea. They could come up at night and let a man ashore in a small boat—"

"Maybe we should look along the shore for the boat," Fiona interrupted eagerly.

"No, they'd just drop him off and go back to the submarine."

"All right. That makes sense. But why *here*?" Alison persisted.

"Maybe he's to look around and report if this would be a handy place for an invasion."

"That's silly, Kathleen. On the *west* coast? Everyone knows the invasion will come across the North Sea. That's why we were sent here, after all," Maureen retorted boldly.

"Oh, that's just their cunning. You said it exactly, Maureen. 'Everyone knows they'll come across the North Sea.' If they put a force ashore along this coast, see, nobody would know it. Then they could march down to Lochgilphead, cross Loch Fine and be on the Clyde blowing up the shipyards in no time at all, and no one in Glasgow would be a penny the wiser until it was too late."

"Oh, my!" exclaimed Moira.

"That makes sense," Peggy chimed in.

"Kathleen, we *must* tell Miss Priestley."

"And have her phoning the police and the army? Why, we wouldn't be let off the grounds till all the fun was over. Come on, Maureen, think! Act like a Magpie. 'One for all and . . .'"

"But this isn't playing, Kathleen. This is real."

Fiona and Shelagh nodded. "Maybe we'd better tell."

"Who says we're playing?" Kathleen's face got red.

"It's not just a game. *We* have to deal with this situation. Don't you see? It's the next magpie. After 'three for a girl' comes 'four for a boy'. The *spy*, just as the rhyme foretold. And it's up to us Magpies to solve the mystery."

"D'you mean for us to catch the spy, Kathleen? But that's dangerous. He could have a *gun*." Fiona giggled nervously.

"Och, no," Peggy put in. "I heard tell they teach spies and the like to kill with their bare hands. He'd not need a gun."

"Oh, Kath, don't let's."

"Fiona, don't be such a baby. There's *eight* of us. He couldn't possibly kill eight of us with his bare hands. Anyway, I'm not suggesting we tackle him head on. We'll keep watch. Look out for anything suspicious."

"Like what?" Alison asked sensibly.

"I don't know yet. We'll know when we see it, won't we?"

"Like the dead rabbit vanishing from under the standing stone," Maureen suggested.

Kathleen's face reddened again. "You know we decided that the stone took the rabbit as . . . as an acceptable sacrifice."

"You don't really believe that, do you, Kathleen?"

"Of course I do. Come on, Maureen. You're a Magpie now. You've got to go along with what we believe in."

No, I don't, Maureen told herself silently. *And you can't make me. It's all superstition and nonsense.*

Then she remembered the stone head, and the threepenny piece shining silvery under the water. Her cheeks got hot. Really, she was just as bad as Kathleen. The only difference was that she wasn't forcing the others to go along with her ideas.

And I didn't leave the offering to placate a power, she told herself again, remembering how she'd worked this difference out. *Only out of a kind of respect.*

Kathleen nodded briskly, as if Maureen's silence counted as consent. "Come on, girls, we'd better get cleaned up for dinner. Tonight, after lights out, we'll think up a strategy to deal with the spy."

As they walked up to the lodge, Fiona said dreamily, "Four of the magpie rhymes have already happened. I wonder when the next one'll come true."

"What is the next one?" Maureen asked. "I forget."

"Five for silver," Kathleen said.

"Och, that could be almost anything." Alison shrugged.

"Come on, Maureen, don't dawdle," Kathleen snapped.

For Maureen had stopped halfway up the slope from the bamboo grove. She hadn't thought of the rhyme Mrs. MacDougall had told her when she'd gone through her pockets, looking for a suitable offering.

But she had just left a silver threepenny bit in the burn below the carved head. *Five for silver.*

CHAPTER SEVEN

"So don't you dare say a word to Miss Priestley about the spy," Kathleen had warned. "Nor to any of the other teachers either."

She must have been reading my mind, Maureen thought wryly. "Oh, all right then," she'd promised reluctantly. But the picture in her mind, like a snap taken with her Baby Brownie, wouldn't go away. In fact, it grew more definite. The memory of the tousled hair, red against the brown-gold of the bracken, the bent back scurrying through the undergrowth, was becoming as clear in her mind as a picture in her album. The picture of somebody who was up to no good.

If only she could get rid of this bothersome image

by telling some responsible grown-up about it. Like Daddy. Or even Mother, when Maureen wrote her Sunday afternoon letters. But she remembered the girls' warning that Miss Priestley read all the mail: "Don't write *anything* you wouldn't want *her* to read." Which didn't leave a lot.

She wondered if Miss Priestly *really* had the time to read *all* their letters home? And, if so, did she read them only to check on the quality of the handwriting and the accuracy of spelling and punctuation? Or did Miss Priestley, like a censorship officer, comb through them for subversive material? Shelagh had received letters from cousins in the armed forces, with bits blocked out in black ink. Places, names or other indiscretions might aid the enemy.

Obviously she hadn't told Daddy or Mother about Kathleen and the Magpies, and certainly not about the standing stone and her own offering at the last full moon. She would have loved to describe her finding of the head in the burn to Daddy. It was something he would have appreciated. But it was *her* secret, certainly not to be shared, however indirectly, with Miss Priestley. The girls' warning had been clear.

She chewed the top of her pen as she sat writing her Sunday letters, and wondered what was left to say.

> Dear Daddy: The weather continues to
> be fine and we are still playing tennis.
> Did you find the *Gallic Wars* boring

when you were at school? I do. Do I
have to go on with Latin after taking the
Junior Oxford exam?

When she had told him about the Sally pudding in
an earlier letter, her story had made him laugh, he'd
said. That was the important thing to remember about
writing to soldiers overseas. Don't worry them; cheer
them up and let them know you are all right. She
crossed out the sentence about not wanting to take
Latin.

"I do miss you. Remember those picnics we used to
take? I look forward to your coming home soon, so we
can go hiking again. Love, Maureen."

It wasn't much of a letter, and she still had to write
to Mother. The same beginning. That was easy. Then
she could tell Mother that she needed more stockings.
In spite of all the darning in the world, her toes kept
poking through the feet. She must have grown. And
she really needed a bra.

She chewed her pen again, wanting to say to
Mother, "I wish you wouldn't go out to dinner and
dances with other men, people who aren't Daddy.
You're not forgetting him, are you?" She doubted that
Miss Priestley would let that through; in any case, she
didn't want the headmistress to know about Mother's
flightiness. And Maureen's words wouldn't make a
halfpennyworth of difference to Mother. "You don't
understand, darling child. It's all part of the war
effort," she would probably write back.

The picture of the stranger in the bracken came back to haunt her, floating in front of her eyes as she stared at the half-empty sheet of writing paper in front of her. *I know*, she thought suddenly. *I could talk to Mrs. MacDougall again*. She remembered the way the dark blue eyes had looked into hers, the feel of the woman's hand on her own. She remembered, too, how sympathetically the older woman had listened when Maureen had visited for tea. Like Gran. Really, she decided, Mrs. MacDougall was the only person besides Shelagh whom she could possibly trust.

She finished her letter to Mother with a large "Love" and a scrawled signature that filled in the lower half of the page, and slipped it thankfully into its envelope. The very first chance she had, she would go down to the factor's house again and unburden herself of her worries.

But finding a chance wasn't easy. Miss Priestley seemed adept at planning activities to keep the students out of mischief. When they weren't in class or study period, there was tennis, hockey and, as the evenings grew shorter, work on a school play for Christmas. "We never have any time to ourselves," Maureen grumbled to Shelagh. She realized for the first time, as she spoke, that this was one of the things she disliked most about boarding school. It wasn't just being away from her friends, or wearing her despised navy uniform, so different from the green and gold of the academy, or even putting up with Kathleen's bossiness. What really bothered her was not having enough time to do what she wanted to do by herself, even if she wanted to do nothing but daydream.

But I *must* get away, she told herself. Later that afternoon, when letters were finished and they were reading parts for the Christmas play, Maureen excused herself. "I just have to go to the loo." She visited the lavatory, so as not to tell a lie, but she didn't go back to the assembly hall. Instead she slipped outdoors, plunged into the darkness of the rhododendrons and ran as fast as she could down to the factor's house.

She was quite out of breath when she got there, her hair tousled by the breeze off the water, and Mrs. MacDougall looked at her in surprise. But then the factor's wife smiled, opened the door wide and said, "Come away in then. I'll set the kettle on for tea."

Maureen sat silently while the kettle boiled, watching Mrs. MacDougall rinse the brown pot, spoon in the tea and pour the water over the leaves.

"It is guid to see you again. We had a bonny visit last time, did we not?" Mrs. MacDougall stirred the tea briskly and poured.

Maureen blushed. "Yes, we did, and I'm sorry. It's been a while since I could get away. Miss Priestley keeps us busy."

"But you got away this evening."

"Yes. I had to talk to you. About something important."

"Aye." Mrs. MacDougall nodded.

There it was again—the feeling that this was a wise woman, one to be trusted, like Gran. Maureen's hand trembled and she put her cup down in its saucer. She struggled to find the right words to tell her story.

"What's bothering you, then?"

"There's the standing stone," Maureen began slowly.

"Aye. Along the shore. From the old times."

"Kathleen—she's the prefect of our form . . ."

"I ken *her*."

"She says it's sacred. That we have to give offerings to it."

The old woman frowned. She put her cup down and almost glared at Maureen. "That's no a guid thing to do. She's a feckless lass, meddling in things she doesna understand. I didna care for her at all. For any of them."

"They're all right, really. But she began a society called the Magpies when they first got here."

"That's an awfu' strange name for a club of young ladies."

"It's because there were seven of them, I think. Before I came. I suppose you told them the rhyme about the seven magpies?"

"I told them too much when they first came here, I ken now." Her face was grim and her fingers clenched her teacup. "They came here, sucking up to me, asking questions, lording over me like the laird never would. He was aye a courteous man, bless him—why, he stood as godfather to our Jimmy." She pointed to the photographs on the mantel. "He gave us that sovereign for a remembrance of the christening day. You can ken why we wouldna spend it, for all we were pinched for pennies many the time." She ran a thumb across the shining coin, as yellow as farm butter. "A 1917 sovereign, it is. Our Jimmy was born on the first of October, 1920."

"Mrs. MacDougall, you were telling me about the girls in my form."

"Oh, aye. I told them more than I should have, I dare say. I do remember telling them the old rhyme about the seeing magpies, the one I told you. I didna think they'd put it to such use." Her voice was bitter as she recited the old lines again:

> One for Sorrow
> Two for Joy
> Three for a Girl
> Four for a Boy
> Five for Silver
> Six for Gold
> Seven for a Secret that can ne'er be told.

Her voice died away and she looked blankly into the smouldering peat fire. Maureen felt a shiver run down her back. Then the clock struck five and the spell was broken.

"They never came back, except with that message from the headmistress when you were with them. Never a gift or a thank you. They've taken what I gave them and turned it into a cheap children's game. It will do them no guid, you can tell them that from me, playing games with the old things." Her face darkened.

Maureen picked up her cup and gulped the strong brew. "I'm part of the Magpies now. I went along with it too," she confessed. "But there's something else I want to tell you about. Something I found by myself in the burn across the moor. A stone head."

The woman's face closed suddenly, like a window slammed shut and the curtains drawn. Maureen held her cup tightly in both hands, as if to warm them up, though the room was stuffy. "I came on it unexpectedly. I haven't told a soul about it. It made me feel . . . I can't describe the feelings. I gave *it* an offering. But I wasn't playing a game, honestly."

Her face changed. "So it was you that gave the blaeberries. Och, aye! On a leaf. MacDougall told me. I was puzzled then who it could be. *Not one of them*, I told him." She nodded and smiled. It was like the sun coming out. "So it was yourself. That was a guidly thing to do."

Maureen let her breath out in a sigh and put her cup down. "I wasn't sure. Because of what the Magpies do. They give an offering to the standing stone at the full moon. Last time they made me do it."

"*Made* you?"

"No, I suppose that's not really true." Maureen sighed again. "I didn't have to. Only I wanted to belong. And I didn't want to seem like a scaredy cat."

"But now it troubles you?"

"The idea of doing it didn't feel right. And what I did afterwards was horrid. Then the sacrifice just *vanished*."

She told the whole story to Mrs. MacDougall, who listened without interrupting, except to refill their cups.

"You say you found a *trapped* rabbit?"

"Yes. We'd seen snares before. Doesn't Mr. MacDougall set them?"

The factor's wife shook her head. "MacDougall isn't bothering himself with snares. He's a crack shot. Never misses. Now who else would be setting snares on the estate?"

"The same person who took the offering, don't you think?"

"Aye. But . . ." A frown creased Mrs. MacDougall's forehead.

"And I think I know who it is," Maureen said eagerly. It came out in a rush of words, and it was like a stone rolling off her back to be rid of the burden at last. "Yesterday I saw someone lurking in the glen to the south of the moor. I *think* I did. A man with red hair and a tweed jacket, going through the bracken as if he didn't want to be seen. Mrs. MacDougall, do you suppose he's a *spy*? And what d'you think I ought to do about it? The girls say not to tell, but—"

She stopped in mid-sentence as Mrs. MacDougall's cup clattered in its saucer, tipped and spilled. The older woman jumped to her feet with a cry and fetched a cloth to mop up the mess. "Och, how could I be so careless? Where are my wits, I wonder?"

She took the cups and set them in the sink to wash. Then she wiped her hands on her apron and turned to look at Maureen.

"Have you told your teachers any of this? Miss Priestley, maybe?"

"My goodness, no. Kathleen said we mustn't. I haven't even said anything in letters to my parents. That's why I came here. I had to tell *someone*. What do you think I ought to do?"

"Do?"

"About the spy? Should I tell Miss Priestley? The police?"

"The *poliss*? I would not be bothering them with this story. Nor your headmistress either. Red hair, you said?" She smoothed her apron with hands that seemed to Maureen a little unsteady. "Och, he'll no be a spy. Just a poacher, after the rabbits."

"Really? That's what you think? So I shouldn't worry about it?"

"No, indeed. Dinna fash yoursel'. I will be telling MacDougall that you were here and were uneasy about it. He'll keep an eye out. As for *her*, you tell her to leave the standing stone alone. No good'll come of her meddling with the old things. You be sure to tell her that now."

"I will. May I come and talk to you again?"

"Aye. I'll be glad of your company. You're a bonny young lady. Not like those others. Come when himself is away. He doesna care for strangers about the place."

"Himself?"

"MacDougall."

"Oh." Maureen paused at the door. "There was one more strange thing I meant to ask you about." She hesitated as Mrs. MacDougall's face seemed to close against her again. "It's about that door in the hillside. The one that's barred and padlocked."

The secret look vanished and the factor's wife smiled. "That? Och, that's just the old icehouse. That's where they used to store the game at shooting parties before the war, you ken."

"An *icehouse*. That's all? Kathleen said it was a dungeon."

Mrs. MacDougall gave a short laugh. "That young lady's got too much imagination for her own good. You'd be better off paying no mind to *her*."

* * *

But it was hard to ignore Kathleen, especially after the temper she got into when Maureen told her what the factor's wife had said about the 'dungeon' in the hillside. "It's just an icehouse. And Mrs. MacDougall says you shouldn't be messing about with the standing stone," she finished.

"What business is it of hers, I'd like to know? And why were you talking to Mrs. MacDougall anyway? Breaking your oath as a Magpie, I suppose. As for paying attention to what *she* says, she's just warning us off the standing stone because she knows how powerful it is. So don't you dare tell the others what she told you, or I'll make life so rotten for you, you'll wish you'd stayed at your own poky school in Saint Andrews."

"I wish that already," retorted Maureen. "I've wished it every day I've been here." She stormed out of the assembly hall and bumped into Shelagh outside. "I wouldn't go in if I were you," she warned. "Kathleen's in an awful temper. All my fault, of course."

"She'll get over it. So long as she gets her own way she's all right. Maureen, where did you get to? I've been looking for you everywhere. They've assigned all the parts in the play and you only get to be a page. Kathleen's the princess and Alison's the prince."

"What a surprise!" Maureen said sarcastically.

"So where did you go?"

"Shh. Is there time to talk before dinner? Come on outside where we can't be heard." She caught Shelagh's hand and pulled her out of the front door and down the slope towards the burn. The Lower Fourth were playing in the bamboo grove and looked resentfully at them, expecting to be evicted, but Maureen led the way over the hill.

"I've been talking to Mrs. MacDougall. There's something I want to show you," Maureen said as they walked up the sandy path. She described her visit, finishing just as they reached the mysterious door in the hillside.

Shelagh drew back. "That place gives me the shivers."

Maureen laughed. "So it should. You'll never guess what it really is."

"A dungeon, like Kathleen said?"

"An *icehouse!*"

"Och, you're joking! Well, no, I guess that makes sense, since this is a hunting lodge. Did you tell

Kathleen? Well, no wonder she's mad at you—it makes her look a right ninny."

"Imagine us believing her. We're all ninnies too. A dungeon!"

"But what about the bar and that great padlock? I wonder why they bother keeping it locked when it's empty."

"To keep out tramps and gypsies, I suppose."

"How many tramps and gypsies have you seen around here? This is the emptiest country I've ever been in."

"There was that red-headed man. But Mrs. Mac-Dougall said he'd be just a poacher."

"That doesn't make a lot of sense. Where'd he come from?"

"*I* don't know. Oh, Shelagh, look at this. Even more mysterious. The padlock's open. We could just unhook it, push open the bar and peek in."

"Do you *want* to?"

"I wouldn't dare. Suppose someone was *lurking* inside?"

Shelagh shivered. "Oh, don't."

Maureen walked slowly by the entrance, staring at the ground.

"What is it?"

"Nothing. That's what's odd. It's all sandy here, and it hasn't rained in ages. But there isn't a single foot-print except for ours."

"Whose would you expect? Oh, I see—whoever unlocked the door. That *is* strange."

"Who'd bother to brush away their footprints? Not Mr. MacDougall, certainly. But suppose it was someone who didn't want to be found. Someone who was *hiding*. Let's look around in the bushes. Maybe whoever was here got careless."

Sure enough, on the slope of hill a few yards from the entrance to the icehouse, Shelagh found a single large shoe print. "A brogue. Well, practically every man wears them, right?"

"Not the factor. He wears boots. And look over here. The sand's a different colour, as if it's been turned over. Someone's been digging here."

"Treasure, do you suppose?"

"A shortwave wireless would be more likely if he *is* a spy. I wish we had a spade."

"There's some in the shed behind the kitchen garden."

Maureen looked at her watch. "No, it's almost dinnertime. Maybe we could dig with our hands. The sand's really soft."

It took them a very short time to dig out the loose fill. "There *is* something here. I can feel it," Shelagh exclaimed. "But not like a wireless. It's soft and . . ."

Maureen had a sudden horrid picture of what might be buried there. "Oh, don't!" she cried out at the same instant that Shelagh picked up a sandy bundle of fur. She dropped it with a scream and it unrolled to disclose the maggoty underside and decayed head of a rabbit.

Shelagh jumped up and rubbed her hands frantically against her skirt. "Och, that's nasty! Oh, dear, I'm going to be sick," she gulped and ran behind a tree.

Swallowing her own nausea, Maureen found a couple of sticks and managed to roll up the disgusting bundle. She pushed it back into the hole and stamped the sand over the top. "Are you all right, Shelagh?"

"Ugh. I suppose so."

"There's the dinner bell. Come on, or we'll be late."

They raced back to the house and shut themselves in the bathroom. Shelagh rinsed out her mouth and they both ran hot water over their hands with no thought of rationing, soaping them over and over.

"Ugh, I can still smell it on my hands." Shelagh shuddered.

"It must be your imagination really, after all that washing, but I do have some perfumed hand cream Mother sent. Maybe that'll help."

They smoothed the cream over their hands and then, as they went downstairs to dinner, Shelagh said slowly, "So Kathleen was wrong about the standing stone. It never took the offering. The spy did. He must have been hiding in the woods all the time you were getting that rabbit and putting it in front of the stone."

Maureen shivered. "That gives me the creeps."

"What should we do? Tell Miss Priestley?"

"I'd have to confess that I was outdoors in the middle of the night and that I stole one of the staff apples."

"What about telling Kathleen?" Shelagh whispered as they went into the dining room.

Maureen shook her head. "Better not. It'll make her

look stupid again and she'll be unbearable. I'd sooner tell Mrs. MacDougall."

"You're late," snapped Kathleen. "What have you two been up to?"

"Not a thing." Maureen unfolded her napkin in her lap.

* * *

The next afternoon, during the play rehearsal, Maureen slipped out of the assembly hall and ran down to Mrs. MacDougall's. *I'm only a page*, she told herself. *I don't have to do anything but stand around. No one's going to miss me.*

As she came out of the rhododendron thicket she saw a battered-looking open car, camouflage-painted, with two soldiers in it. They had obviously just left the factor's cottage. She stopped and watched them bump along the track towards the Oban road.

So that's all right, she thought. *The MacDougalls have told them about the spy. Now I don't have to worry.* She almost turned back. Her errand seemed pointless, and she didn't want to risk being late for dinner again. But maybe the factor should know about the icehouse being unlocked. So she continued down the path and knocked at the door.

The factor himself opened it. "Aye?" Maureen drew back from his unfriendly look.

"I was just . . . I wanted to see Mrs. MacDougall, please."

"Who is it, Angus?"

"One of the young ladies." He spoke over his shoulder, filling the doorway with his bulk.

There was a sigh. "You'd best let her in then."

He stood aside reluctantly and Maureen squeezed past him into the front room. The factor's wife seemed to have aged ten years. Her face was drawn and her eyes sunken in her head.

"I . . . I didn't mean to disturb you," Maureen stammered. "I came to tell you . . . but then I saw the soldiers, so I knew you'd already told them."

"What would we have been telling the soldiers?" The factor stood over Maureen.

"Just about the man I saw in the valley. The man with—"

"The soldiers came about something else entirely," Mrs. MacDougall interrupted. "I didna see fit to bother them with hearsay. Something that might well be a young lady's imagination."

Maureen heard the warning in the woman's voice, but chose not to heed it as her own anger rose. "I *didn't* imagine it. And I came to tell you that I found the icehouse unbarred."

"Did you go inside?"

"No, we were scared."

"We?"

"Shelagh and I. But we found the buried remains of that rabbit I told you about. The rest had obviously been eaten. Don't you think it must have been that man I saw, the man with—"

Again Mrs. MacDougall interrupted her. "Thank you for telling us, Miss. MacDougall will be looking to lock the icehouse." Maureen found herself being forced back towards the door.

"Goodbye then," she said awkwardly and fled up the path, wishing she had never gone.

In the few minutes she had spent in the factor's cottage the sun had vanished and the sky had clouded over. The loch was pewter grey, sullen, and a sharp wind had got up. She shivered. What had turned Mrs. MacDougall into a hostile stranger? There had been no current of unspoken understanding between them today. Instead Maureen had felt as if the woman had been fighting her, willing her to leave.

And why had the soldiers been there? Nothing to do with the supposed spy lurking in the bracken, Mrs. MacDougall had said. But why would two soldiers have driven all the way from Oban, if not about national security?

The thicket seemed even darker than usual, the lurking shadows between the great bushes more menacing. Maureen felt her flesh creep, and she kept her eyes steadfastly on the path ahead of her and her mind on the lights of the lodge, which she would surely see in a minute. In spite of herself, panic seized her and she began to run, stumbling over roots that snaked across the path. At last she saw the turrets and crowstepped gables. She ran around to the front, across the gravel and into the warmth and light of the great hall.

It wasn't dinnertime yet. Someone was inexpertly banging on the grand piano in the assembly hall and someone else was stumbling over her lines in the play.

"Where *were* you?" Shelagh hissed in her ear. "I tried to cover for you, but Kathleen's on the warpath. She doesn't like Magpies going off and doing things on their own."

"Oh, bother Kathleen!"

Shelagh giggled. "Hush. Don't let the others hear you. Come on, take your place, page!"

As Maureen obediently climbed onto the stage, her mind was still going over that strange scene in the factor's cottage and Mrs. MacDougall's odd behaviour. Twice she had interrupted Maureen, just when Maureen had been about to mention that the stranger in the bracken had red hair. It was almost as if Mrs. MacDougall had known what Maureen was going to say and was determined to stop her. But there had been no one else there but the factor. Whose greying hair had once been red. But why?

CHAPTER EIGHT

"I have received a very disturbing complaint from the kitchen staff," Miss Priestley announced after the formal assembly the next morning. "Canned food and bread are missing from the pantry. Though I find it hard to believe that any of the young ladies of Logan Academy could be guilty of such an act, it is difficult to imagine who else might be responsible."

Maureen felt a quiver of totally irrational guilt shiver through her body. *Don't let me blush*, she prayed. *Don't let Miss Priestley look at me*. She felt like standing up and shouting, "I stole an apple!" but clenched her hands instead. She glanced at the other Magpies. They were all sitting very still, their eyes downcast.

Miss Priestley went on talking. "And with food shortages, and the fair play that shortages demand, for one of you to take more than your share is particularly reprehensible. I hope that sometime during the course of today the guilty person will see fit to come and see me. If I have *not* received a confession by tomorrow's assembly, then I shall be forced to take disciplinary action that will affect all of you, the innocent as well as the guilty." She swept out and, in the stunned silence that followed her announcement, Miss Cavanagh dismissed the students.

"Do you suppose it could be the man I saw in the bracken?" Maureen suggested as they made their beds. She went on, forgetting that she and Shelagh had decided not to tell the others of their grisly discovery. "He had to skin that rabbit and cook it. Ugh! I think he must have been really hungry to do that, don't you? So breaking into the kitchen at night to get a decent meal or two would be worth the risk."

"What *do* you mean—he ate the offering?" Alison stared, and Maureen had to explain how she and Shelagh had found the horrid remains. Kathleen's face flushed. "That isn't so. I told you—the stone accepted the offering."

"And skinned it and ate it, I suppose," Shelagh interrupted. "You can't have it both ways. Either we believe in the spy Maureen saw, which makes sense of the vanished rabbit *and* the robbery in the kitchen. Or we have to believe in the spirit of the stone, which is pretty silly, considering Maureen and I both saw the rabbit's remains."

The others nodded agreement and looked at Kathleen.

Maureen watched Kathleen's expression change. First a hot flash of anger, then a glare at Maureen between narrowed eyes—*if looks could kill*, Maureen thought—and finally a smile, pasted over the other emotions like wallpaper over a cracked wall. "Perhaps you'd better ask Maureen to be leader," she said sarcastically.

"That's silly," Maureen said quickly. "Look, Kathleen, I don't want to argue with you about the stone. It's not the real issue. What are we to do about this man who may be a spy? Shouldn't we tell Miss Priestley, especially since the food has been pinched from the kitchen?"

"You know what she'd do if she thought there was a spy wandering about out there? She'd cancel all outside activities. She'd keep us under her eye every minute; we'd practically be prisoners. She'd say it was just for our own good. For our safety. And then we wouldn't stand a chance of catching the spy ourselves."

"But shouldn't we tell the police? Or the army? It's their job, after all."

"Don't be so wet, Maureen," Alison broke in. "Kathleen's right. Imagine being stuck in the house or being supervised outside every blessed minute. It's boring enough now."

The others nodded. Kathleen said quickly, "We'll vote on it. All in favour of keeping quiet about the spy and doing our own investigation, hands up." Every hand went up except for Maureen's and Shelagh's.

"Passed," said Kathleen triumphantly. "So you two have got to promise not to tell. All right?"

They nodded reluctantly.

"Good. Not a word to anyone. As soon as class is over I'm going to ask Miss Priestley for permission for the Lower Fifth to explore the woods and the moor."

"Suppose she won't let us?"

"Don't worry. I'll come up with a good reason."

* * *

As soon as Miss Urquhart had set their homework and swept out of the room, Kathleen whispered triumphantly to the class, "It's all right. We've got permission to go up in the woods."

"However did you wangle that?" Moira gasped.

"Especially with Miss P. in a temper about the food robbery!" added Peggy.

"Never you mind. Collect your blazers and come on."

The eight Magpies were just trooping across the main hall when Miss Priestley came out of her study. "So this is my keen botanical group? Miss Urquhart will be most impressed, I'm sure. Remember to note the habitat of the specimens you collect. And, above all, no tasting! I don't want to have to explain away a case of fungus poisoning to your parents." She nodded and glided majestically up the main staircase.

As soon as the front door closed behind them, the girls turned on Kathleen.

"Whatever did you say?"

"What *was* she talking about—fungus poisoning?"

Kathleen giggled. "I had to think up a good excuse, one I knew she would approve of. So I said we had decided to do a project on our own, investigating the different kinds of fungi that grow in the area. She loved it."

"But that's daft," objected Fiona. "We're going to have to come up with specimens."

"She's right, Kath. Miss Urquhart's going to be waiting with bated breath for our great display in class tomorrow morning," Alison added.

"It'll be a bit of extra work, I realize. But think about it. It's a great excuse. We're going to have to search the whole slope for clues." She waved her hand at the wooded hill across the burn. "Just like police looking for a missing person."

"But what *are* we looking for?" Peggy asked. "The spy's not going to hang around waiting for us."

"We'll look for anything that might be a clue. A footprint. A hidden wireless. And while we're doing *that*, we'll keep an eye out for fungi."

"That's pretty good, Kath," Fiona said admiringly.

"Of course it is. You can trust *me*."

The message was unspoken but clear: *I am your leader. I and no one else.* Even though Kathleen wasn't looking at her, Maureen knew that the other girl was waiting for *her* reaction.

"Brilliant," she said, and felt Kathleen relax. "Where'll we start?"

"At the icehouse."

"You mean the dungeon, don't you?" Shelagh asked with pretended innocence.

"Oh, that was just my joke. I knew perfectly well it was an icehouse all the time." Kathleen managed a convincing laugh.

Maureen nudged Shelagh in the ribs. "Don't goad her, silly."

"Well, you don't have to suck up to her either," Shelagh hissed back.

"I'm just being political."

"Come on, you two," Kathleen called. "Don't dawdle. I've got pencil and paper for all of us, so we can make a note of where we find a particular fungus."

"Where'll we put them?"

"Oh, stuff them in your blazer pockets. They'll be all right."

When they reached the icehouse, the bar was once more slipped over the hasp in the frame, and the padlock was locked around it. *The factor must have come up last night and closed it*, Maureen thought. *After I told them about it.*

Kathleen gave the padlock a tug. "No one hiding in there, anyway. All right, all of you. Spread out along the bottom of the wood and work your way slowly up. See what you can find."

"There's a footprint right there." Alison pointed.

"That's the factor's," Maureen said after they had all crowded around. "He was wearing boots like that yesterday."

"Take a look, everyone," Kathleen instructed them, "so if you see it again, you'll know it doesn't count."

They separated and slowly climbed the slope. Maureen found a leathery flap of fungus on the trunk of a tree, broke it loose and wrote "on larch tree bark" on her paper.

There was a shout from her left. "There's a rabbit snare here."

"Any footprints?"

"Not a one. It's all been smoothed out. Wait, here's one!"

They scrambled across the hill to look. "Definitely a man's brogue. Not the factor's boots. Good work, Peggy. Now we know Maureen's not just been seeing things. There definitely *is* a stranger lurking on the estate. All right, everyone. Spread out again."

They met at the top of the hill without discovering any more clues, other than another footprint, which they guessed was made by the same pair of brogues.

"But two footprints aren't much to go on," Shelagh said. "We still don't know if he's a spy or a poacher."

"I can't imagine anyone bothering to come all the way out here to poach rabbits. You couldn't make a living at it. Anyway, all the people around here, like Mr. MacDougall, shoot what they need for the pot. They don't fiddle around with snares. And why would anyone come here to poach? Goodness knows, there are rabbits all over Scotland."

As if to prove Alison's point a rabbit scuttered out

almost from under their feet, sprinted across the moor and vanished into the bracken.

"We won't find footprints up here and there's nowhere to hide. Maureen, why don't you show us exactly where you saw the man."

Maureen pointed out the place. "Down in the valley to the south, where the bracken's thick. And he was moving to the left." She pointed towards the plantation of pine and larch that covered the hillside to the east and south.

"He'd have to have a source of fresh water, wouldn't he?" Alison said. "Even more important than food."

"There's the burn near the icehouse," Maureen suggested.

"That might do at nighttime, but not in the day. Half the windows at Kintray Lodge overlook that burn. That's a good point, Alison. Let's walk south and see where all the water on this moor drains to."

Oh, no, thought Maureen in sudden panic. *They'll find the burn. And then the stone head.* Somehow, keeping it secret was as important to her as finding the spy. What could she think of to distract them?

"Come on, Maureen, don't lag behind. This is *your* spy we're hunting, after all."

Reluctantly she followed the others. They found the burn straight away and followed it down the slope.

Maybe they won't see the head hidden under the grass. I almost didn't.

Fiona went by, followed by Eileen, Moira and Peggy. But Alison's sharp eyes didn't miss it. "Look over here. There's something shining in the burn."

Seen from above, the head looked like nothing but a weathered stone. What had caught Alison's eye was below it, lying in the water beside the threepenny bit that Maureen had left, glowing through the water like a marsh marigold. A gold coin.

As Alison knelt, ready to scoop it from the water, the three girls farther down the slope looked back to see what was going on.

"There's a face in the burn!" yelled Moira.

"Look at those bulgy eyes. Weird!" added Peggy.

"And a smiley sort of mouth. Och, it looks scary, like it's watching us." Fiona shivered.

The others scrambled down to look. Only Maureen lingered above, reluctant to share what had been her private discovery.

"It looks awfully old. I wonder how long it's been here?"

"As long as the standing stone, maybe."

"I wonder who knows about it but us?"

"Whoever put those coins in here." Alison pushed up the sleeve of her blazer and dipped her hand into the burn. "Criminy, the water's cold!"

"Don't!" Maureen exclaimed, but it was too late. Alison's hand came out dripping.

"Don't what?"

"Take away the coins. Don't you see, they're offerings. *Real* offerings. Not like the games we played with the standing stone."

Kathleen flushed angrily. "The stone *isn't* a game.

Don't listen to her, girls. Come on, Alison, let's have a look."

The others crowded round. "It's a gold sovereign!"

"How could anyone lose a sovereign in the burn?"

"Not lost, I told you. Put there." As she spoke Maureen had a sudden flash of memory. On the mantel above the fireplace in the factor's cottage had been photographs. A wedding picture of the MacDougalls. Family photographs. Pictures of a baby. And beside them a gold sovereign.

Given by the laird as a christening gift to the boy. Well, you can ken why we wouldna spend it. She could almost hear Mrs. MacDougall's voice.

"Look at the date," she said clearly above the excited chatter of the others. "It should be 1917."

Alison turned over the coin in her hand and peered at it. "1917 it is. How on earth did you know that?"

Maureen found that she had been holding her breath. Now she let it out in a sigh. It was all so clear. The two soldiers from Oban. Mrs. MacDougall's unhappy face after they had gone. Her reaction when Maureen had first described the red-haired man on the moor. The factor's bottled-up rage. And now the coin offered to the stone head. A cry for help.

She held out her hand. "It belongs to Mrs. Mac-Dougall. I'll take it back to her."

Alison's fingers closed over it. "Oh, no, you won't. Finders keepers."

"Not when you know the rightful owner." Maureen went on holding out her hand. Alison hesitated.

"If you don't give it to me, I'll tell Miss Priestley," she threatened.

"It's not fair. I saw it first."

"Oh, give her the rotten coin," Kathleen snapped. "But that's it, Maureen Frazer. I'm fed up with you. You're out of the Magpies and that's the end of it. Come on away, girls."

The Magpies. Maureen looked down past the stone head to where her threepenny piece still glinted through the water. "Five for silver," she said aloud, and then stared down at the sovereign in her hand, with St. George slaying the dragon embossed on one side, the old king's head on the other. "And six for gold," she whispered, feeling the weight of the coin in her hand and its chill from the water of the burn.

She walked slowly downhill to where she could see the stone head, its eyes staring blankly across the valley, a secret smile on its face. She shivered. *Six for gold.*

"Just coincidence," she firmly told the bulging eyes. Then she climbed back up to the top of the moor and slowly followed the seven down towards Kintray Lodge. Then she hesitated. Coincidence or not, "six for gold" had solved the mystery. She decided not to wait another minute. Instead of following the others across the grass and into the lodge, she went straight ahead down the path through the rhododendrons that led to the factor's cottage.

Mrs. MacDougall opened the door and stood with her hand on it, blocking the way. "What would you want with us again, miss, disturbing our supper?"

"It's important." Maureen held out her hand, the sovereign on her palm.

Mrs. MacDougall's eyes closed and she seemed to shrink, to become suddenly older. "I suppose you'd better come in," she said grudgingly and turned, with Maureen following her.

A quick glance told her that the room was empty, though the teapot was keeping warm on the stove and there were two plates with fried sausages and mashed potatoes on the table. She looked towards the mantel. "You've put away his photographs?"

"Angus did that after the soldiers were by."

"He deserted, I suppose," Maureen said gently. "He'd be the red-haired man I saw down in the valley. He trapped rabbits for food and slept in the icehouse. And after the soldiers were here looking for him, you put the sovereign in the burn."

"I thought if anyone could save my boy it might be the old ones."

"I'm afraid it's too late for that, Mrs. MacDougall. He's stolen food from the school kitchen. Miss Priestley is bound and determined to find out who's responsible."

"I'll pay her for anything he took," the factor's wife said proudly. "For I suppose, now you know, you'll be telling her."

Maureen hesitated, twisting her fingers together. "I don't know what's best to do."

"Then leave well enough alone, lass, I beg of you. He's only a young lad, just turned nineteen. He joined up before war broke out, to chum his best friend. He didna really ken what it was all about. Not till they started their training. He wrote to me what it was like. They were made to do bayonet practice, running at sacks stuffed with straw, hanging up like they were human beings. The sergeant had them pretend the sacks were real people—Nazis, I suppose—and they had to push in the bayonets and twist them, like they were twisting the blade in the men's guts." Mrs. Mac-Dougall put her hands over her face. "They had to yell and pretend to hate them. He said it made him sick. He said he couldna do that to another human being. He told me in his last letter that he didna ken what to do."

"Did you know he'd actually run away?"

The factor's wife shook her head. "Not till the military poliss came looking for him. They didna believe that he hadna come home. I ken well enough they'll be back. And what will they do with him if they catch him? They can shoot a man for desertion in time of war. Did you ken that, lass?" She stifled a sob. "He hasna been here. We've not seen hide nor hair of him. But when you told me you'd spied a red-haired man hiding in the bracken—he has a bonny head of hair, has Jimmy—and you'd found the rabbit snares, then I knew he'd come back. He used to set snares when he was a wee lad. Always so proud when he could bring me a rabbit for the pot on his own. Och, he was always such a brave wee lad. I dinna ken what'll happen to him now. The shame of it! Och, you willna be telling on him, will you, lass?"

Maureen turned away from the pleading face. She twisted her hands together. How had she got herself into this terrible predicament? "I . . . I don't know, Mrs. MacDougall," she stammered. "I don't know what's the right thing to do. There's a war on. It . . . it changes the rules kind of, doesn't it?"

The heat of the peat fire and the cookstove, the tightly shut windows, the pain she saw on Mrs. Mac-Dougall's face—suddenly Maureen felt sick and dizzy. She staggered towards the door and pushed it open, gulping in the fresh air, shivering at the cold wind off the sea.

She turned back to where Mrs. MacDougall still stood in the middle of the small room, her hands clasped together as if she were praying. "I'll think about what's best to do," she promised. "That's all I can do. Goodbye."

She turned away and began to walk fast, south-wards, along the shoreline where the meadow met the loch, where coarse grass and sea pink gave way to barren rock and seaweed. She remembered walking this way with Shelagh, right after Geoff Drummond had died. He'd been in the armed forces too. A young officer drowned on duty watch. Would *he* have run away, if he'd known what his fate was going to be? She thought not.

But then Jimmy MacDougall wasn't a privileged deck officer on a great battleship. He was only a private in the army, one number among thousands of others, and his job was to kill the enemy in a much more direct and messy way. It would be much harder for Jimmy, wouldn't it?

On the other hand, there *was* a war on. What could Jimmy do but fight? He was in the army, what other choice would he have? Suppose people like Daddy, in the reserves, had refused to go to France when they were called up. Who would protect everyone against the invading Nazis? What would happen then? Hitler—and crazies like him—would take over the world.

"I just don't know what to do," she said aloud and stuffed her hands into the pockets of her blazer. Her fingers found the remains of the fungi she had picked earlier that very afternoon—a time that seemed a hundred years ago, when hunting a spy was just a lark. When the red-haired man didn't have a name or a family.

Striding along, paying no attention to what was around her, Maureen was startled to find that she had walked almost as far as the standing stone. Close by was the path leading to Kintray Lodge. She'd have to go back soon. She'd have to make up her mind whether or not she was going to tell Miss Priestley the truth, not so that the students wouldn't be punished for stealing food from the kitchen—that would be selfish—but for a more important reason. Something to do with Geoff Drummond's death at Scapa Flow, with Daddy and all the men like him, on alert somewhere in France. And with all the other men and women who were involved in the war effort. Something to do with fairness, with balance.

Maureen found herself thinking of the head in the burn, wishing that she could find an answer in those blank eyes, that enigmatic smile. But at heart she knew the ancient stone could not help her. The old ones were only for the Stone Age people, the people who had erected this standing stone, who had hunted the wild boar long before the invading hordes had come to these islands. Before the Romans, the Saxons, the Vikings, the Danes and then the Normans. Before Hitler.

As these thoughts rolled round and round in her head, Maureen automatically turned up the path that ran over the wooded flank of the hill to the south of the lodge. The closer she came to Kintray Lodge, the more the need to make up her mind—to make *some* kind of choice—weighed on her.

What am I to do? Keep silent? Or tell Miss Priestley and leave the responsibility up to her—the responsibility of telling the police and the army about Jimmy? She stopped abruptly, her hands digging into her pockets.

I can't tell on him, she thought. Absentmindedly she took the fungi from her pockets and threw them on the ground. Playing games, hunting spies, pretending to work on a botany project—all of it now seemed so stupid. The hard reality was a young soldier who was afraid and had tried to run away from his fear, but had unwittingly brought the fear and disorder with him. *How can I tell on him?*

Maureen listened, but heard no answer in the quiet evening. The wind soughed gently through the trees;

there was no other sound. Then, startlingly close at hand, a dry stick snapped with a noise like a gun shot. She jumped and looked over her shoulder, quickly but not quickly enough. Through the dusky shadows she saw a blur of movement. Then something rough was thrown over her head and shoulders and her hands were pulled behind her back.

She tried to scream, but choked on dust. She tried to pull away, but the grip on her wrists was too strong. She lashed out with her feet, but whoever was holding her kept behind, out of the way of her kicking.

She felt herself being pushed forward and, to avoid falling over, she had to walk obediently where she was led. Stumbling along in the dark, stifled and blinded by whatever covered her head, she could only sense that she was being led uphill. The lodge—and safety—must be only five minutes away. Was anyone outside? Or were they all indoors by now? Surely someone would see her and come to her help. She yelled again, but her voice was muffled in the folds of the covering and the dust made her choke helplessly.

Then she was suddenly yanked to a stop. She could feel her captor close behind her, fumbling for something. She heard the scrape of metal on metal. A click. A metallic clatter. As her mind translated the sounds into pictures, she began to kick and struggle again in panic.

But it was too late. She was pushed forward and felt herself falling, farther down than she'd expected. The jolt as her feet touched ground jarred her spine and she fell on her hands and knees with a grunt. As soon as she had recovered from the shock she tore off the covering on her head—it felt like a potato sack—but she was no better off. Her eyes met only blackness.

Behind her she heard the iron bar slam over its hasp. She heard the click of the closing padlock. Then there was silence, as profound as the darkness. Under her knees the floor felt like sand. Around her was the dark, earthy smell of underground.

Kathleen had been right after all. The icehouse *was* a dungeon.

CHAPTER NINE

Maureen began to yell and then decided that yelling was stupid. Everyone would be indoors by now. Soon it would be dinnertime and at least then she would be missed. She could imagine Miss Priestley asking where she was and Kathleen answering. But that was the catch! Kathleen wouldn't tell the truth. She wouldn't say that Maureen had been expelled from the Magpies, that none of them would speak to her or notice her, much less care where she was.

No, Kathleen would probably say something like, "She's a difficult person, Miss Priestley. She's never really fitted in, however hard we tried to make her welcome. Always wandering off on her own. I expect that's what she's done, Miss Priestley. Gone off on her own and forgotten the time."

Of course the other Magpies would back her up. That's what they were all about, weren't they? Follow-my-leader. All except Shelagh. Maureen could always hope that Shelagh would be worried enough about her to do something. But night fell fast at this time of year. If no one took her absence seriously until after dinner, there wasn't much Miss Priestley could do. Not till morning.

At the thought of being trapped in this dank prison for the next twelve hours or more, Maureen felt panic rising in her throat. She wanted to scream, but bit her lip and hugged her knees to her chest. If only one of the girls would confess the truth to Miss Priestley and tell her that Maureen had probably gone to take the sovereign back to Mrs. MacDougall, then the head-mistress would have a lead. The factor's wife would be able to tell them that she'd seen Maureen walking back along the shore towards the standing stone. That information would help narrow the search, she told herself. But this imagined sequence of events wasn't a whole lot of comfort.

"Let's look around," she said aloud, and was startled by the dead sound of her voice in this space. "Looking" was a joke, of course! The icehouse was blacker than any place she'd ever been in before.

She got cautiously to her feet and walked forward, her hands outstretched. Roughly finished wooden planks met her fingers. *The door*. She braced herself

and pushed, even though her brain told her that pushing was futile. She could still remember the definite
click of the padlock being snapped over the hasp.

She slid her hands down the rough surface. At the
level of her shins the wood came to an end and her
fingers encountered the damp feel of raw earth. It
took her a moment to realize that the icehouse must
have been dug downwards as well as into the hill. In
the old days, when they had hunting parties here, the
space up to the level of the door would have been
filled with blocks of ice covered with straw.

Cautiously she turned to her right, keeping her left
hand on the wall. After only half a dozen tentative
steps her foot encountered something soft. She froze
and drew back, remembering with a shudder the soft
fur of the dead rabbit. But when she bent down, her
cautious hands felt only wool cloth. A musty blanket,
stiff with dirt, folded in two to make a bed.

She dropped to her knees beside it and groped
around. She found a small pile of hard objects, both
squarish and cylindrical. Tins of something? A pillar
shape, slippery smooth—could it be a candle?—and,
next to it, a small box that rattled with the comfort-
ably familiar sound of matches. Yes! Thankfully she
struck one, lit the candle and held it aloft, her eyes
momentarily blinded by its little flame.

It was amazing how the enormous black void
shrank down to a room smaller than the dorm. On the
right was the door, as unyielding to her eyes as it had
felt to her hands. To her left tree roots had intruded

from above, dangling trails of hairy rootlets. She shivered, thankful she had found the candle before encountering them. In the flickering light they had a faintly sinister look, like goblin fingers. In the dark they would have been terrifying.

Beside the blanket, which looked almost as disgusting as it had felt, Maureen could see the mysterious objects, now revealed as oblong tins of corned beef and round tins of stew. There was also part of a loaf of bread, a bit mouldy, a knife, a spoon and a tin-opener. *At least I won't starve before they find me*, she thought more cheerfully.

In the centre of the floor were the remains of a fire. That must be where Jimmy MacDougall had cooked the rabbit he had taken from the standing stone. There had been no sign of a fire outside. She found herself shaking and realized that it was cold and damp in the icehouse, the kind of cold that slowly penetrates the bones.

She pulled together the charred pieces of wood and added some broken sticks from a pile in the corner. It wasn't until she had actually struck a match that she realized a fire would be a death trap. With the door closed, the smoke could not escape and, in any case, the fire would eat up the oxygen in the room, oxygen she must conserve to survive. The door was a close fit. Not the smallest line of light had shown around its edge.

She blew out the match, shook out the filthy blanket and, stifling a shudder, wrapped it around her like a cloak. Then she squatted down with her back against the dirt wall, opened a tin of corned beef and hacked off a slice. The knife wasn't very sharp and made a mess of the loaf of bread, but she cut away the mouldy bits and made a satisfyingly thick sandwich with the rest.

The meat was a bit salty, but the sandwich took away the edge of her hunger. She ate as slowly as she could, chewing thoughtfully, savouring each mouthful and making it last. Making the time pass.

When the small meal was over, she sat still, her knees hugged to her chest. In spite of the sandwich there was still a hollow feeling in her stomach. Fear; the awful fear of *not* being found, of staying in this tomb-like place until it actually became—a tomb. Would dinner at the lodge have begun yet? Had her absence been noticed? She shivered and bit her fingers.

The saltiness of the beef left her with a thirst and she could do nothing to slake it. Outside her prison, no more than a few yards away, the burn trickled down to the loch. Clear, cold refreshing water. *Don't*, she told herself firmly. *You mustn't think about how thirsty you are. It's mostly your imagination anyway.*

But what else was there to think about? She could lie down and try to go to sleep; that would pass the time. But suppose someone *should* come by, calling her name? Suppose she were asleep and didn't hear the voice? Suppose the person went on past the ice-house and didn't come back?

No, don't think like this, she rebuked herself. She tried to imagine that she was David Balfour, running away from the English soldiers. What would he do in this predicament? Or Daddy, what would *he* do? Imagining Daddy as her companion was a lot more comforting than conjuring up the hero of *Kidnapped*.

He would never panic, not Daddy, she told herself. *And neither will I.*

She straightened her back until she was sitting bolt upright against the wall. She took a deep steadying breath and stared at the candle flame. It burned without flickering, a flame of gold drawn upwards to an unwavering point, with an oval of brilliant blue at its heart. When she stared too hard it turned into two flames, with two hearts of blue. She blinked. A pool of wax suddenly breached the rim and ran wastefully down the side. How long would the precious candle last? It seemed to be the only one.

Regretfully she blew it out. There might be a time when she needed it more than she needed it now. The dark rushed in, blacker than it had been before, so dense that it was almost suffocating. She licked her lips and began to sing softly all the silly wartime songs she could remember.

Singing about "Hanging out the Washing on the Siegfried Line" made her think of Mother, helping to win the war in London, and dining and dancing with glamorous officers at the Ritz and the Savoy. She thought about Daddy, somewhere in France. Maybe he was on duty right now, watching the stars come out one by one over some little village on the frontier. So very far away.

She wished she hadn't thought of stars. She automatically looked up into the awful blackness above her head. She could feel it pressing in on her from the walls and roof, stifling her.

Was the air getting stuffier or was that just her imagination? How long could a person go on breathing in an almost air-tight room? She yelled "help" a couple of times, but soon gave up. Her voice sounded so muffled that she didn't believe it could possibly penetrate the door to the real world of stars and moonlight out there. And perhaps shouting would use up the air faster. She swallowed panic and tried to make herself breathe slowly, evenly, so as not to waste one precious molecule of air. Would someone ever come?

* * *

"So all we have to go on is a couple of footprints and a sovereign. It's not much, Kath."

"But it *is*, Peggy. The sovereign is a real clue. Spies often travel with gold instead of currency. I suppose it's easier to spend in different countries."

"Not in the west of Scotland, I should think," Alison said bitingly. She was still annoyed at Kathleen for letting the new girl take the coin from her. "Imagine trying to use a sovereign to pay for a pair of kippers or some finnan haddie in a fishmonger's in Oban!"

"In any case, Kathleen, Maureen said the sovereign belonged to Mrs. MacDougall. It has nothing to do with the spy," Shelagh argued.

"Well, if you want to take *her* word for that . . ."

"So you successfully concluded your investigation . . ." Miss Priestley's voice cut into the Magpies' conversation at this inappropriate moment. They stared at each other, mouths open. Fiona gave a nervous giggle. ". . . into local fungi," the headmistress concluded.

"Oh, the *fungi*," Kathleen said breathlessly. "Yes, thank you, Miss Priestley. After supper we intend to get together and assemble our collection."

As Miss Priestley nodded her head and moved off graciously to talk to the Upper Fifth, Peggy let out her breath in a whistle. "Whew! I thought she meant—"

"We all know what you thought, Peggy," Kathleen cut in. "We'll talk about *it* while we put our specimens together." She looked at her watch. "Have any of you seen Maureen? She'll be late for dinner if she doesn't get a move on." The bell rang. "There now. She *is* late. Well, I for one refuse to take any more responsibility for her. Come on, girls."

"You really were awfully mean to her, Kathleen."

"She was prepared to betray the Magpies, Shelagh. I had no option." Kathleen frowned as she pulled out her chair and sat down. "You'd better watch out or you'll be in the same boat. Please pass the bread, Eileen."

"Someone is tardy." Miss Urquhart loomed over their table, her hands on the back of the empty chair. "Maureen. Where *is* Maureen, girls?"

Kathleen broke the uneasy silence with a dramatic sigh. "She has this tendency to wander off on her own. I *have* tried . . ."

"Wander off? You mean she is not in the house? But it is almost dark." Tutting, Miss Urquhart bustled off.

"Here comes Miss P.," Fiona muttered. "Trouble, trouble."

"Not if we all stick together," Kathleen whispered quickly. "Let me do the talking." She turned in her chair with a suddenly anxious expression on her face. "Miss Priestley, we came in ages ago. I thought Maureen was with us then. She must have done one of her disappearing acts."

"Disappearing acts?" Miss Priestley repeated, frowning. "She seemed a very steady sort of girl to me. I wasn't aware . . . Who saw her last? Come on, girls. Speak up."

"She was definitely behind me coming down the hill towards the burn," Eileen said slowly.

"Close behind?"

"Well, not exactly. A wee bit behind."

"Did you look back and talk to her? No? Did any of you talk to her on your way down the hill? No one? No one at all?"

Cutting through the guilty silence, Kathleen smoothly explained: "We were hurrying, so as not to be late for dinner. I don't think any of us stopped to chat, not until we got up to the dorm and began to wash and tidy up for dinner."

"And was Maureen with you girls then?"

Silence.

"Do any of you have the *least* idea where she might have gone?"

"She did say that she wanted to talk to Mrs. Mac-Dougall," Shelagh said, avoiding Kathleen's glare.

"This late in the evening? Kathleen, you are form prefect. Why did you not dissuade her?"

Kathleen shrugged, her face suddenly sullen. "She wouldn't listen. She didn't want to cooperate, Miss Priestley. She just doesn't fit in."

"Hmm." Miss Priestley glanced at her watch and then looked anxiously out of the dining room window at the gathering dark. She sighed impatiently. "It is quite ridiculous that there are no phones out here."

"Miss Priestley, please may I run down to the factor's cottage and see if I can find her? It's not quite dark yet."

Miss Priestley hesitated. Then she nodded briskly. "Very well, Shelagh. But by no means alone." Her eye ran over the seven, pausing at Kathleen, then moving on. "Alison, you will accompany Shelagh. Take coats, girls. It will be chilly out. And make sure you both have torches. And come straight back!"

"Yes, Miss Priestley."

As the two girls set off around the driveway towards the north, Alison grumbled, "Why me? Dinner'll get cold."

"It's your honest face, Alison."

"Oh, whisht!"

As they entered the rhododendron grove they both fell silent. There was something ominous about the darkness of the thicket. Their torches made only small circles of gold on the path ahead of them and above the looming shrubbery the sky was almost as black. One star twinkled. The moon had not yet risen.

Shelagh shivered. "Suppose the spy's out there?"

"Do shut up. Why did you have to be such a goody-goody and volunteer anyway?"

"If you hadn't been such a greedy pig about the sovereign none of this would be happening."

"Greedy pig, yourself," Alison replied automatically. "Och, what was that?" She clutched Shelagh as a pale shadow glided over their heads.

"Whisht! It's just an owl, silly. Come on."

They walked as fast as they could out of the thicket, almost running by the time they came to the meadowland. Under the open sky it was not as dark, though the land was grey and black and empty-looking. They ran down the path and pounded on the door of the factor's house.

Silence.

"Maybe no one's home."

"That's silly. Where'd they be away to? Anyway, I can see the lamp between the curtains. And the fire's going. I can smell the peat smoke." Shelagh hammered again.

The door opened a crack. "Who is it?" It was the factor. A tall man and broadshouldered, he filled the space.

They shrank back. Then Shelagh stammered, "We're looking for our friend, Maureen Frazer. You know, the new girl."

"She's not here the noo." He began to close the door.

Desperately Shelagh stuck a foot in the crack. "She

said she was coming to talk to Mrs. MacDougall. Almost an hour ago. She *told* us. And she hasn't come back."

"She *was* here." Mrs. MacDougall spoke from behind her husband's shoulder. The admission seemed reluctant. "It was a bit ago. She stayed but a wee while and then left."

"Which way did she go? Up the hill through the rhododendrons?"

"'Tis the quickest way, isna it?" Again the factor made to shut the door, but his wife stopped him, her hand on his arm.

"No, Angus. She didna go that way. Maybe you didna see. You were in the back room when I was talking to the lassie. She walked back along the shore."

"Towards the standing stone?"

"Aye. That way." Mrs. MacDougall hesitated. She looked from Shelagh and Alison to her husband and back again. "Are you saying that the lass is lost?"

Shelagh nodded. "She didn't come home for dinner. No one's seen her. We'll go back that way. Maybe we . . ."

"It's awfu' dark out there. You could fall and hurt yourselves. Better that MacDougall go with you. He knows—"

"Hold your tongue, woman, why can't you?"

"If the lass is lost, Angus, you *must* go. You have the big lantern. See them safe home and be looking for the young lass too along the way."

The factor grunted and silently, grudgingly—it seemed to Shelagh and Alison—led the way along the shore. He walked fast, the lantern casting a golden light on the tufts of sea pink, the tangles of black seaweed. The two girls followed behind, the small beams of their torches dancing to and fro, lighting up in turn the dark rocks, the foaming sea, the rough grass.

"Suppose she's drowned?" Alison whispered.

"Och, shut up. Don't be so daft. She wouldn't go near the edge." Shelagh's voice rose almost hysterically.

The factor strode along, his boots sure on the slippery stones and tussocks of rough grass, while Shelagh and Alison stumbled after him, almost running to keep up. At the standing stone he stopped and waited for them, swinging his lantern so that the shadow of the stone fell to the south, to and fro, like the pendulum of a great clock.

"Doubtless she'll have turned up towards the house by the path yonder." The factor pointed uphill. "There's no sign of her hereabouts."

The two walked in silence behind him until they came to the fork in the track.

"No, wait!" Shelagh called after him as he turned left. "She wouldn't have gone that way. She'd have taken the path to the right."

Reluctantly the factor turned. "How can you be sure? Well, maybe you should be taking this path to be sure, and I'll hasten up the other one. That way we'll know, will we not?"

"I *know* she'll have gone this way, the way she went before," Shelagh said obstinately. There was something in the factor's manner that set her on edge. "She'd never choose a new path in the twilight, one she'd never been on before, especially when she was hurrying to be in time for dinner. It doesn't make sense."

She set off determinedly along the righthand fork, her torch scanning the ground ahead of her. "Look, Alison. What's this?"

"Those are just pieces of old tree fungus," the factor said, kicking them out of the way. "Nothing to do with the young lady. Let's hurry on to the lodge. I'd best see what Miss Priestley would have me do." He strode ahead of them again, his lantern swinging.

"But what were *tree* fungi doing on the ground?" Shelagh asked.

"She must have emptied them out of her pockets. At least it proves she *did* come this way," Alison said sensibly.

"But why would she have done that?"

Alison shrugged. "Tired of carrying them, I suppose. For goodness' sake stop asking stupid questions, Shelagh Drummond. Come on, the factor's way ahead of us."

"There's no other sign of her. Do you suppose she could have been kidnapped?" Shelagh asked breathlessly as they caught up with MacDougall.

"Now who would be doing a thing like that?" The factor turned to wait for them. "Or is the young lady maybe an heiress?" His voice was mocking.

"I shouldn't think so. But suppose . . . Oh, Alison—" Shelagh dropped her voice to a whisper. "Suppose she found the spy. Or the spy found *her*. Remember what Peggy said: they can kill you with their hands, just like that. He could have killed her and dropped her in the loch or in the bog so she couldn't tell on him."

"That's a lot of nonsense, like in a film, not real life." Alison's usually calm voice shook. "You don't believe it's a spy, do you? Not really?"

* * *

"A spy? Really, Shelagh, what on earth are you talking about?"

They were in Miss Priestley's study, the factor standing awkwardly by the door in his boots, Alison and Shelagh sitting on a sofa facing the headmistress. The girls looked at each other in silence.

"Well?"

Then out tumbled the story of the man Maureen had seen.

"Spies? Hidden radios? Really, girls, this is too much. We are trying to find one of your form mates who is lost, who may be in difficulties with a twisted ankle or some such predicament. This is no moment to spin a wild romance! I don't think you realize how serious this may be."

"But we do, Miss Priestley, honestly. Maureen saw him. The spy, I mean. Maybe he saw her too and that's why—" Shelagh choked and burst into tears.

"Och, there's no spies, Miss Priestley," the factor said. "Maybe a poacher now and then."

"Then where can she have gone?" Shelagh burst out.

"There's no telling. Not till daylight. If it's your wish, ma'am, I'll be up to the lodge early on the morn's morn for your orders."

"Thank you, Mr. MacDougall. First thing in the morning then. We must consider getting in touch with the police in Oban. Oh, for a telephone!"

She turned to the two girls as soon as the factor had left the room. "Now, girls, obviously a lot more has been going on than you have yet told me. Perhaps something may shed light on Maureen's disappearance. So speak up. The whole story, please. I'm going to get to the bottom of this rigmarole if it takes all night."

* * *

"Magpies? You told her about *that* too?" stormed Kathleen.

"You wouldn't ask that if you'd been there. Honestly, Kathleen, talk about the Grand Inquisitor!"

"And the standing stone? And the offerings?" Fiona groaned. "I suppose you told her about me sneaking out in the middle of the night? She'll kill me!"

"Actually, she wasn't that interested. She was more interested in Maureen's offering—the rabbit, I mean. And about Shelagh and her finding the remains. I'm sorry, Kathleen, but she *made* us tell." Alison twisted her hands together.

"Made you? I can't believe that you'd break your solemn oath, just like that!"

"Aren't you all forgetting about Maureen?" Shelagh screamed at the others. "You're all so selfish, worrying about getting into trouble with Miss Priestley, and all the time Maureen could be lying dead or something." She burst into tears again.

The other Magpies looked at each other in silence. Shelagh stared defiantly at Kathleen and blew her nose. "It's all your fault!"

"That's not true," Kathleen stammered. "It was all a game, after all, wasn't it? Just a game to pass the time. To make the Duration bearable."

"Bearable for us, but . . . Goodness, you don't suppose she was so miserable she tried to run away and fell in the bog?" Moira gasped. "You were rather awful to her, Kath."

Kathleen's face went white. "Don't talk like that!" she snapped. "Why'd she go up the hill if she were running away?"

"That's true," Alison agreed. "If she really were running away she'd take the coast path to the Oban road and try to get a ride, wouldn't she?"

"But that's just as bad." Moira also burst into tears. "In the dark she could have missed the path and fallen into the sea. The current could have got her."

"The big whirlpool, the Corrievreken," Peggy added.

Kathleen's hand went to her mouth. "I don't believe it. She wouldn't be so stupid." She jumped off the four-poster and ran over to the chest, pulling out Maureen's drawers.

"Look, see here, all of you. Her purse is here. Her gas mask. Her identity card. She'd never run away without them, would she?"

There was silence.

"Well, would she?" she challenged.

"I suppose not."

"We know she walked back along the shore from the factor's cottage and up the path towards the lodge. Mrs. MacDougall saw her leave and you two found the fungi that she'd emptied out of her pockets. So we know she got *that* far."

"But why did she empty her pockets?"

"Maybe it was a sign. Like 'X marks the spot'. Like the breadcrumbs the children left in the forest. It was close to the icehouse." Shelagh stopped suddenly and put her hands over her mouth. "The *icehouse*," she gasped. "Stupid! Why didn't I think of that before? I'll bet that's where she is. We've got to tell Miss Priestley right now."

"Come on, girls!"

They clattered down the stairs and Kathleen pounded recklessly on the door of the headmistress's study and flung it open, not even waiting for an answer.

"Young ladies, *what* are you thinking of?" Miss Priestley rose to her feet, frowning majestically. She had been sitting on the sofa beside Mrs. MacDougall, whose face was stained with tears, a crumpled handkerchief clutched in her hand. "Leave the room at once. I will speak to you later."

"But it's important, truly," Shelagh burst out. "We think we know where Maureen is. In the *icehouse*."

Mrs. MacDougall's face cleared. She burst into tears. "The icehouse! Why did I no think o' that? Aye, that's where he'll ha' hid her. Oh, thank the good Lord! She'll be safe enough there. I was afeared."

"*Safe?* Locked up in the dark? The poor child will be out of her mind with fear. Mrs. MacDougall, have you got the key?"

The factor's wife shook her head. "There was a spare, but it's been mislaid for years. MacDougall has the only one I know of."

"And you don't know where he is now?"

She shook her head. "He'll be out looking for Jimmy to give him money and get him away from here before the morn's morn."

"Then we must manage as best we may. There must be some tools about the place. A crowbar perhaps? A large screwdriver? Come, Mrs. MacDougall, pull yourself together. I need your help. We must get the poor child out of there before this upset turns into a tragedy."

"'Tis a tragedy already. What's to become of my Jimmy?"

Miss Priestley patted her hand. "We will worry about that later. Come now, Mrs. MacDougall. Show me where we're likely to find some useful tools."

"In the shed next the kitchen garden, ma'am. Everything will be there."

Miss Priestley swept towards the door, stopping to

scan the seven girls crowded there. "Bed," she said brusquely. "I will speak to you all in the morning."

Once the two women had left, the Magpies looked at each other. "Bed's hopeless at a time like this," Shelagh said slowly.

"It'll take them ages to find the right tools," Fiona added.

Kathleen nodded. "Right. Come on, Magpies."

They slipped out of the house and ran down past the burn and into the darkness of the trees. "Anyone bring a torch? Bother. Just be careful not to twist an ankle on a tree root."

The icehouse loomed up among the trees, a dark hump of hillock. Kathleen tried the padlock and pulled at the bar. It held firmly.

"You know, I think it's going to take more than a crowbar to open this. It's built like the Bank of Scotland!"

Shelagh hammered on the door with her fists. The heavy planks seemed to absorb the sound. "Maureen, can you hear us?" she yelled. "We'll get you out soon. Hang on." She put her ear to the door and listened. "I can't hear a thing. Oh, suppose she *isn't* inside."

"She *must* be," Kathleen snapped. "Let's all yell together. One . . . two . . . three . . . MAUREEN!"

They waited, listening.

"Suppose she's already . . .?" Moira's frightened voice broke the silence.

"No, she can't be!" Kathleen pounded on the door

again. "MAUREEN!" She stifled a sob. They listened again.

A twig cracked.

"You'll be wanting the key." A quiet voice spoke out of the shadows.

Fiona and Moira screamed. They all turned in time to see a dark shape dislodge itself from the shadow of the trees and resolve into the figure of a young man in ill-fitting shabby tweeds. He held out his hand to them. On the palm lay a rusty key.

"Are you . . . are you the *spy*?" Fiona's voice trembled.

"Spy? What are you on about? There are no spies around here. My name's Jimmy MacDougall."

Kathleen grabbed the key and, with shaking hands, pushed it into the lock. It turned easily with a satisfying click. She pulled the padlock open and unhooked it from the hasp.

"Here. I'll give you a hand with that bar. It's uncommonly heavy."

The bar dropped and the door swung slowly open.

"Maureen, are you there?" Kathleen peered into the darkness, the others crowded close behind her. "Maureen, please talk to us. Are you there? Are you all right?"

A pale face blinked up at them from below knee level. Kathleen stretched out her hands. "Grab hold, Maureen. I'll haul you up."

* * *

Maureen had drifted into an uneasy doze and a horrible dream in which the standing stone was stalking her across the moor. Its shadow fell across her and, in the dream, she screamed. She woke with a start. A clang of metal rang in her ears. Part of the dream? No! A crack of grey light appeared in the blackness, a long streak, a whole rectangle. The night outside her prison was almost dazzling. This must be how an owl sees, she thought, blinking. She waited, silent, wondering whether it was her kidnapper again and, if so, what he was going to do with her. She bit her lip and clenched her fists so the nails dug into the palms of her hands.

"Maureen, are you there?" It was Kathleen's voice, but timid and trembly—not like Kathleen at all.

Maureen let out her breath in a gasp. She licked her dry lips. It was all right. She wasn't going to die.

"Maureen, please talk to us. Are you there? Are you all right?"

She managed to croak out an answer and struggled to her feet, blinking up at the pale faces swimming in the darkness above her. Two hands reached out. "Grab hold, Maureen. I'll haul you up." It was Kathleen's voice again.

Then she was out of her prison in the blessed fresh air. The Magpies were hugging her. Crying. And she was crying too and hugging them back. Even Kathleen. Kathleen was hugging her so hard Maureen was breathless. "You're all right? Really all right?"

Then she saw him. One shadowy figure standing

aloof. In the faint starlight his red hair looked almost black.

"You're Jimmy MacDougall," Maureen said bluntly. Just like his picture on the mantel.

"Aye. You'll be fine now, I reckon. So I'll be off."

Maureen caught his hand as he turned away. "Don't go. Don't run. It's not worth it."

"I ken that. I'm not running. Not any more. I'm off to Oban to give myself up."

"MacDougall? You're the factor's son?" Kathleen interrupted. "Your mother's up at the lodge. She'll be on her way here with Miss Priestley any minute."

"There's the light of them coming now." Eileen pointed down the track. Jimmy tensed and turned.

"No, wait." Maureen still held onto Jimmy's hand. It was icy cold and clammy in hers. "Your mother'll want to see you before you go."

"Will she? Do you think so?"

"Of *course*."

"Well, maybe . . ."

"Yes, stay, Jimmy. It'll be all right, I promise."

They all turned to meet the two hurrying up the hill.

Miss Priestley stopped abruptly. "Really, girls! I distinctly said 'bed', did I not?"

"But we got her out. She's all right. Look." Maureen was pushed forward into the glare of the torches. As the group was lit up Mrs. MacDougall gave a cry.

"Och, Jimmy!" She ran into his arms.

"He had a key. He helped us get Maureen out," Kathleen said.

"Well, I daresay that's a point in his favour." Miss Priestley's voice was cold. "But I'm afraid it will not go well with you, young man. Running away from training camp might be excusable. After all it is not, as I told your mother, like deserting in the face of the enemy. But to kidnap an innocent child and lock her up in such a place—"

"But he didna." Mrs. MacDougall turned to face the headmistress. "You dinna understand. It wasna Jimmy that took the child. It was MacDougall himself."

chapter ten

The strange evening ended for Maureen in a very commonplace and cosy way, with cocoa and sandwiches in Miss Priestley's sitting room. Mrs. Mac-Dougall and Jimmy sat close to each other on the sofa. The factor's wife could not take her eyes off her son, Maureen noticed, and kept reaching over to stroke his arm as if she couldn't quite believe that he was real.

Maureen concentrated on eating. It was amazing how hungry she was, considering that she had had a corned beef sandwich not many hours before. Perhaps fear made one extra hungry, she thought, and reached out for the last sandwich at the same moment that Jimmy did. They smiled at each other and drew their hands back.

"You take it," Maureen said. "You must be starving."

"Och, it was no so bad. It was sleeping out and not having a good wash once in a while I minded. And the fear of being spotted. That was the worst."

Meanwhile, as they ate and drank their hot cocoa, Mrs. MacDougall was explaining more of the story to the headmistress. "I had nae inkling that Jimmy'd run off, not till the young lady told me that she'd seen a red-headed man hiding in the valley. Then the military poliss came in from Oban, asking us when we'd last seen Jimmy, when we'd last heard from him. They didna take our word for it, but searched our wee house like we were criminals. Now you couldna hide a babe in there, much less a grown man, so they went off. But I ken'd they didna really believe us, that they'd be back."

"You must have been desperately worried about your son."

"Aye, ma'am, that I was. At my wits' end. And himself—MacDougall—he was mortified. 'The shame on our name,' he said. 'The shame to the laird's name. We must never tell a soul.' And he made me swear on the good book itself that I wouldna say anything about Jimmy." She sighed. "He's a good man, but hard when it comes to his honour."

"Then I found the sovereign and brought it to you," Maureen put in. "So you knew that I knew about Jimmy."

"The sovereign? That I do *not* understand, Mrs. MacDougall." Miss Priestley frowned.

The factor's wife twisted her fingers together and blushed. Jimmy put his hand over hers. "You've got to understand, ma'am, that Mum's family has lived in these parts for nigh on ever, you might say. They believe in the old things, the old ways."

Maureen saw the puzzlement still in the headmistress's face and tried to explain. "It's a bit like Catholics lighting a candle in church when they've got a problem. It's like calling attention, or giving an offering."

"An offering? But that is idolatry." Miss Priestley put down her cup and sat stiffly upright.

"We all have our own ways, ma'am," Mrs. MacDougall said. "Yours are different, coming from a big city in the east, I dare say. A new sort of place."

A small smile cracked Miss Priestley's rigid face. "Hardly new, Mrs. MacDougall. Saint Andrews is one of the most ancient cities in Scotland. Why, the city goes back to the tenth century."

"A thousand years old?" The factor's wife nodded. "Aye. Like I said—new."

In her mind's eye Maureen again saw the stone head gazing southwards across the valley with its blind, bulging eyes. She knew exactly what Mrs. Mac-Dougall meant. She had had a small glimpse of that ancient world when she had sat on the hillside imagining a Stone Age landscape, its wild forests and wild boars.

"So when Alison found the sovereign in the burn," she explained to the headmistress, "I recognized it as

Jimmy's christening present from the laird, that Mrs. MacDougall had shown me. And of course I knew she must have put it there. So then I guessed that the 'spy' we'd been looking for must really be Jimmy."

"Keeping that information from me—*that* was really naughty, Maureen. Naughty and reckless. My blood curdles to think what might have happened to all of you if he really *had* been a spy."

"Yes, Miss Priestley," said Maureen meekly, and then had to bite her cheeks to stop from smiling as Jimmy winked at her.

"But I interrupt your narrative. Please continue, Maureen."

"So I took the sovereign back to Mrs. MacDougall and told her I knew about Jimmy. And she told me about the military police being after him."

"And I begged her not to tell on him, ma'am. MacDougall was in the back room. I knew he must have been listening to her, and I didna know what he might do to protect the laird's honour and his own too. I was worried for the girl when she wouldn't say outright yea or nay, whether she would tell on us."

"I just didn't know whether to keep quiet or tell you everything, Miss Priestley. I was in a muddle and I just didn't know what was the right thing to do. So I walked back along the shore, trying to think it out."

"And MacDougall went after her." The factor's wife took up the tale. "He wasna gone long. When he came back he just said, 'She won't be telling on Jimmy,' so I thought he'd persuaded the young lass. But later in the eve the other two lasses came down to tell us she was missing. Then I was feart for her." The factor's wife swallowed. "When himself came back from seeing them safe to the lodge, I asked him, 'What have you done?' But all he'd say was, 'I'll no have a MacDougall publicly disgraced, not on the laird's land.' And he took all my bits of savings from the tea caddy on the mantel. So I knew he was going to give them to Jimmy and get him away from here. I asked him, 'Is the lass safe home then?' and he said she wasna. 'Not till Jimmy's awa',' he said. But he wouldna tell me what he'd done with her." She gulped back a sob.

"I still don't see why he had to grab me and lock me in the icehouse. It was so horrid." Maureen shivered at the memory.

"I didna ken that's what he'd planned, lass, or I'd have been after him, honour or no. I'd never have let him do such a thing. But when he said you weren't safe home I was feart he'd done something to stop you telling and I daresn't think what it might be. So as soon as he'd left again I ran up to the lodge to talk to Miss Priestley here." She mopped her eyes with a damp handkerchief.

"Dinna fret, Mum." Jimmy patted her hand. "It's over the now." He turned to Miss Priestley. "Dad had guessed earlier the place where I'd be hiding out. When I was a bairn I used to play in the old icehouse, times when hunting parties weren't up. But he closed the padlock against me, so I knew it was his way of warning me to stay away. That was all right. I had another hidey hole, a cave down by the old beach that goes back to the old times, the Stone Age times, they reckon. That's where Dad found me this e'en. He gave me the money and told me to get out. He said nobody knew I'd been there, naught but a lass from the school. He told me he'd locked her in the icehouse, and he'd let her out once I was gone down to England."

"But you didn't go. You stayed and helped get me out. That was really brave, wasn't it, Miss Priestley?"

"I couldna let him do that. It was him locking you up that told me just how wild he was with me. That made me stop running, in spite of the money he'd gi'en me, and start thinking again. I knew I couldna run for the rest of my life. And I couldna disgrace my family. Och, it was a gey stupid thing to have done, running away in the first place."

"It was awfully brave of you to stay," Maureen said again. It was important that Miss Priestley should take Jimmy's courage into consideration. She turned back to Jimmy. "But where did you get the key for the padlock? Surely Mr. MacDougall didn't give it to you?"

"I already had it." Jimmy smiled. "I suppose Dad must have forgotten. I'd had the spare key since I was a bairn. I'd an old tin cigarette box full of the sort of treasures that bairns collect. It was hid at the back of my cave. It was finding it there put me in mind of the icehouse. So I took my old blanket and bits and pieces and hid there until Dad warned me off. It was a sight warmer and drier than the old cave." His face reddened. "And I stole food from your kitchen, ma'am.

I'm sorry. I'll pay you back for what I took, I promise you that."

"That's all right, young man. I am sure you would not have taken it except in desperation. You've been through a great deal," Miss Priestley went on, "and I think the best thing now would be for you to stay the night here, in the lodge, so there'll be no more trouble with your father. Then in the morning I myself will drive you to Oban. I'm sure if you give yourself up to the authorities it will be a mark in your favour. And I will certainly give you a positive character reference."

"In spite of my stealing your food, ma'am?"

"As I said before, the circumstances were exceptional." She smiled. "As for you, Mrs. MacDougall, I thank you most sincerely for coming to tell me that Maureen might be in danger. It was brave of you to stand up to your husband like that."

"Och, I couldna have slept a wink worrying about the poor lassie." She sighed. "A'weel, there'll be wounds to heal and it'll a' take time. He's a gey proud man, is MacDougall. She hesitated. "It was a foolish thing he did, but it was for the laird's honour, not just his own. You will not be holding it against him?" She looked anxiously at Miss Priestley.

The headmistress looked grave and, before she could answer, Maureen interrupted. "Please, Miss Priestley, don't tell the police or the laird. I'm all right, really. And I'm sure he wouldn't have done it if he'd had time to think. It was just as much my fault for not telling you about my seeing Jimmy in the bracken."

"I . . . really . . . I can't think what your mother and father would say."

"But you mustn't worry them about it, must you? There's a war on." Maureen brought out this cliché triumphantly and, to her relief, saw Miss Priestley's mouth twitch in a reluctant smile.

"Perhaps it would be wisest to let sleeping dogs lie," she said. "But I must speak to the factor in the morning, Mrs. MacDougall."

"I will tell him. And I thank you, ma'am. I'll say goodnight to you then and be on my way." She stood up stiffly and bent to kiss her son on the forehead. "You're a good lad, Jimmy. Will I be seeing you in the morn?"

"We'll stop by the cottage on the way to Oban," Miss Priestley promised.

As Mrs. MacDougall left, Maureen suddenly remembered. "Why, that's the seventh magpie!"

"What are you talking about, child?"

"The counting song Mrs. MacDougall gave us." She recited the verse:

> One for Sorrow
> Two for Joy
> Three for a Girl
> Four for a Boy
> Five for Silver
> Six for Gold
> And Seven for a Secret that can ne'er be told.

"That was it, you see, Miss Priestley. Jimmy was the secret that couldn't be told. Isn't it amazing? But it's all turned out all right, so maybe magpies are lucky after all."

Miss Priestley looked severely at her. "Some magpies, perhaps. But a certain eight Magpies will report to my study directly after assembly tomorrow. Then we'll see about 'luck'. Now off you go to bed. You've had quite enough excitement for one day."

* * *

Even Miss Priestley's threat couldn't upset Maureen. She snuggled down in bed and began to count her blessings. Daddy's last letter had said he was well and safe. Mother was winning the war in London in her own way. And maybe that was all right too. *I have to learn to trust her*, she told herself firmly. *I know she really does love Daddy and me. I'm sure in my heart that she wouldn't do anything to hurt us. Maybe I could try being nicer to* her. *I have been a bit of a brat at times.*

As for the Magpies, she thought, turning on her side and closing her eyes, they really were 'all for one and one for all' at last. They'd shown that when they'd rescued her. Even Kathleen. *Especially Kathleen*, she corrected herself, remembering how Kathleen had hugged her and afterwards, away from the others, had whispered how sorry she was for all her meanness. Yes, Kathleen had had a good fright and she'd be a nicer person for it.

As for the standing stone, well, that's all it was, an ancient stone on the shore of a western sea loch. And the carved head in the burn? *Still my special secret*, she thought. *But the old ones are not for me. I've got the Duration to live through, along with the others. Some day peace will break out and Mother and Daddy and I will be together again, and then we can get on with the rest of our lives.*

Until then I've got the Magpies. I know we'll all be special friends now, not just for the war, but forever. And I'll never forget this first autumn at Kintray Lodge, when the eighth Magpie flew in among the Seven.

Chapter One

The dream was back again. As before, it had been rain-ing, but now the rain had turned to sleet, freezing slush that clung to the windshield wipers. Dad had slowed down and was hunched over the wheel, peer-ing through the small arc of visibility at the dark road ahead. Mom was beside him. Joan was sitting in the back seat, half asleep, idly watching the red tail-lights of the semi ahead of them. In the dream, she knew that something terrible was about to happen.

The lights of the semi suddenly moved violently, improbably, from right to left and back again. She heard her mother cry "Max!" and in the same second felt the car swerve left as Dad desperately tried to avoid the jack-knifing trailer. In slow motion, the car scraped the concrete median. In slow motion, she saw the back of the trailer slash sideways, like the tail of an enormous dinosaur, flattening the BMW against the concrete. In the dream she screamed and tried to run, to get out of the way of the dinosaur, but, as is the way in nightmares, her legs wouldn't obey her brain. She felt as if she were trying to run through molasses.

She screamed again and found she was sitting up in bed, her brain still saying "Run!" while her legs lay like two cylinders of heavy clay, refusing to obey. *Just like the dream*. Her nightgown was soaked with sweat and her scream echoed in her ears. Had anyone heard her? She held her breath, listening to the quiet house settle around her. If she'd wakened Dad with her yelling, he'd fuss and make another appointment with the "trick cyclist." As if talking to a psychiatrist would help. She didn't want to *talk*. She just wanted the dreams to go away and the feeling in her legs to come back.

Footsteps in the hall. So she *had* wakened someone. She bit her lip. She could hear soft slippers shuffling. That was all right then. It was only Mrs. Middleton, the housekeeper.

"Are you all right, Miss Sandow? I thought I heard . . ."

"It was nothing, Middy. Just a stupid dream."

"Uh-huh?" The bedside light was switched on. "Why, you're drenched! Come on, let's get you out of that nightie and into a dry one before you get a chill." Mrs. Middleton bustled around, opening and closing drawers, lifting Joan so that her nightgown was freed from under her hips and she could wriggle out of it and into a fresh one. Her pillows were vigorously punched.

"Like a mug of warm milk? No? Are you sure? It's no trouble . . . I guess you'll be all right then."

"Thanks, Middy. Middy, don't tell Dad."

"Well, I don't know . . ."

"*Please*. I'm sorry I woke you."

"That's no problem, my dear. You know that. Sleep well now."

After the door had softly closed, Joan lay on her back staring at the ceiling. The moon must be up, for the room was filled with patterns of light and dark where the thin curtains shifted in the breeze. She imagined getting out of bed, walking over to the windows. Maybe opening the French doors and running across the dew-wet grass under that full moon. She had never done that in the old days, before the accident. But if she had wanted to, she *could* have. Tears trickled from her eyes and ran down into her ears.

Quit that, she told herself. *Be thankful you're still alive.*

Big deal, another voice inside her said bitterly. *You call this living?*

If only the dream didn't keep coming back. The worst part of the nightmare wasn't just reliving the crash over and over, with that small, never-to-be-forgotten flash of Mom, crushed to death in the front passenger seat. That was bad enough, but worse was that, even in the dream world, her legs wouldn't work.

[3]

Even in her dreams, she was no longer able to walk or run. It wasn't *fair*.

"So you're stuck in a wheelchair," one of the counsellors had said briskly. Too briskly. "Sure, it's not fair. But it's a fact. And you're going to have to build a new and worthwhile life around that fact."

"Like how?" she had asked rudely.

"Like going back to school, for a start. Like getting on with the rest of your life."

High school. She'd imagined the impossibility of going there already. In detail. Lockers out of reach. Swinging doors slamming into her chair. Unclimbable stairs. Trying to navigate immensely long corridors with everyone staring at her. People doing things for her, not because she was tops, *numero uno*, admired as a star athlete, but because they were sorry for her, because without them she was helpless.

"*School*? No way!"

"Think about it," the counsellor had urged at the end of the session. "You've got to make a life."

She was ready to battle the point about school, but in the end she didn't have to. Dad was on her side from the first, arguing with the counsellor. "You have no idea just how cruel and thoughtless young people can be. I won't have them hurting my princess." And that was it. Argument over, and she'd won. She felt almost cheated. Had she been looking for more of a fight, maybe being *forced* back to school? She wasn't sure. Anyway, she wasn't going to get a chance to find out, because Dad fixed everything.

In fact, refusing to attend high school in a wheelchair was the last of a series of decisions she had made, almost without meaning to. She'd made the first decision when she was still in hospital and her friends had come to visit her. She still shrank from the memory of them clustered around her bed, some of them embarrassed into silence, the others chattering away and giggling as if there were nothing serious the matter with her.

Their behaviour had seemed horribly callous at the time, though now she understood that they had simply been trying to find a way of handling the situation. But after their visit, she had shouted at Dad, "Don't you ever let them in here again! They stared at me as if I'm some kind of freak show."

He'd arranged it—as he'd arranged everything she wanted—with a notice saying No Visitors. It hadn't stopped Patty Earle. She and Patty had been best friends right through from Grade One till they got on the swim team together. When the nurses wouldn't let Patty in, she'd phoned, not once, but day after day, until Joan had screamed at her.

"Stop asking me how I'm doing today. What do you think?"

"I think you're crazy, Joan Sandow, if you want to know. Creeping into a hole the way you're doing."

"It's no business of yours. Why don't you get out of my life like everyone else?"

There'd been a silence at the other end of the line, and Joan had felt a twinge of something like guilt.

Then Patty had said quietly, "Any time you want to talk, Joan, I'll be here. You've got my number." And she'd hung up. Joan had put off calling back to apologize until it was impossible, and another door had swung shut.

Once out of hospital, she'd begun a new kind of life in the big house on the hill, as splendidly alone as a princess in a palace. Well, that was her choice, wasn't it? She reminded herself that she had everything she needed. Nancy Carter tutored her in her high school subjects every morning. Three afternoons a week, Kathy came to give her physiotherapy and massage. Dear Max had spared no expense, and he gave her what time he could spare, which wasn't a lot, since MaxCom Industries took up most of his time.

The emptiness was unbearable. But when she'd begun to explore the Internet, things had changed. She'd got involved in a chat room discussion about competitive swimming and, almost before she'd realized what she was doing, she'd started to talk about her times and the particular warm-ups that she felt were most helpful.

But this isn't true, she'd told herself, staring at the message she'd just sent. *Not any more.* And the great black hole of misery had begun to suck her back in. But a question had come back, intended for *her*, and she'd suddenly realized that nobody out there knew she hadn't been able to swim a length since May. Nobody knew that she was a fifteen-year-old has-been stuck in a wheelchair, or that she'd never swim again.

Nobody on the Net knew. No reason why they should ever find out. "I can be whoever I want to be," she'd said to the monitor. "Whoever. Whatever." And a giggle had bubbled up unexpectedly from somewhere deep inside her.

"I won't be Joan Sandow any more," she'd decided. "I'll be . . . Joanna. Yeah . . ." And she had begun to type in an answer, imagining this new person. Joanna was a warrior kind of name, for a black-haired long-legged all-round athlete and competitive swimmer, with a sharp brain in the same package. Not that different from what she had been before the semi had destroyed her life.

She had begun a tenuous kind of friendship with a swimmer from Australia, who lived in an upside-down world where Christmas was in the summer and the sun shone in the north. Her Net name was Anti, short for Antipodes, she'd said, and she worked as a physiotherapist in a Sydney hospital.

But even though Joan's days had started to pass less slowly, the nightmares still came. Not every night, but often enough for her to dread going to sleep. Like tonight. She stared at the moonlight moving across the curtain for what seemed like hours.

*   *   *

"Good morning, Princess," Max greeted her as she wheeled her chair into the dining room the next morning. "Sleep well?"

"Yes, thanks, Dad." She avoided Mrs. Middleton's eye as the housekeeper put a bowl of cereal and fruit in front of her. Mrs. Middleton didn't exactly wink, but almost. Joan wished that Dad wouldn't still call her Princess. It was a carry-over from the days when she could run and dance, when she took ballet lessons and dreamed about being another Karen Kain in *Swan Lake*, before she gave up that particular ambition in favour of the dream of winning a gold at the Olympics. It had been a cute nickname when she was small, but now, fifteen years old and imprisoned in this chair, it was ridiculous.

One day, she had written a story on her word processor about a princess with no legs, but it didn't work out the way she'd planned it. When the princess kissed the frog it jumped up and hopped away and she couldn't run after it. So Joan hadn't written any more stories.

In her new disguise as Joanna, she'd begun to explore the Net. Some of the people out there were really weird, and she'd backed out of a few chat rooms in a hurry.

They're not real people, she'd found herself thinking. *Just screwed-up heads. I want to meet someone real. Something like a friend.*

You had friends, a small bleak voice had reminded her. *But you shut them out.*

I want a new kind of friend. One who won't pity me. Fat chance!

Then, one evening, she'd seen the notice.

LOOKING FOR CHESS PARTNER. HIGH SCHOOL.
STRICTLY AVERAGE.

The address was whizkid@Freenet.edmonton.ab.ca.
Yes! Joan had thought. *A new kind of friend. And somebody local. Not weird and way out.*
She'd left a message on his e-mail.

HI, WHIZKID. I CAN BEAT MY DAD ABOUT FORTY
PERCENT OF THE TIME. THE REST HE SLAYS ME.
WHAT'S YOUR FAVOURITE OPENING?
joanna@maxcom.ca.

It was true about beating Max. What she hadn't said was that he hardly ever had time to play, what with running one of the smartest software companies in the country, and that she'd beaten him when his mind was on some incredible program his designers were working on. But the message had got the response she'd hoped for.

HI, JOANNA. GLAD TO MEET YOU. I'M FREE MOST
EVENINGS TILL SPRING WHEN THE BASEBALL
SEASON STARTS. HOW ABOUT YOU?

Joan had been typing in ALMOST ANY TIME when she'd realized what it would sound like. Like she didn't have a life. After all, as Joanna, she was in high school, a competitive swimmer, and *very* popular. How much time *did* she have?

NOT A LOT OF FREE TIME. LET'S TRY FOR A
SESSION LATE IN THE EVENING AND SEE HOW
FAST WE MOVE.

It had been a beginning, but it hadn't been enough.

"I've got this buddy on the Net," she'd told Max after a few weeks. "But playing chess by e-mail's kind of slow."

"What's wrong with the phone, Princess?" Max had smiled at her.

Joan's hands had clenched the arms of her chair. What was wrong was that a phone number would give away the possibility of an address, of Whizkid finding out that she wasn't Joanna.

"Uh-uh." She'd shaken her head. "No way is he going to know I'm a cripple."

Max's smile had vanished and his face had sagged. He'd looked a lot older since the accident. Since Mom's death.

She'd swallowed. "Sorry, Dad. I shouldn't have said . . ."

"Don't worry about it, Princess. Let me think. Hey, why don't I give this friend an account at MaxCom? Then you can 'talk' to each other in real time?"

"That'd be fantastic! Thanks a lot, Dad."

*   *   *

Chess was just the beginning. She had a friend. They'd played computer games in tandem. Whizkid was pretty smart at these, but Joan had the edge on him because she could spend a lot of time during the day figuring out possible moves.

Then Max had given her a jigsaw puzzle at Christmas, a black-and-white print by M. C. Escher that pictured a house with not just one "up" and "down," but three ups and downs, inhabited by people living in the different dimensions, unaware of each other's existence. It was a wicked challenge. Which staircase belonged where? Should this man's head point to the left or the right or straight up?

YOU SHOULD TRY IT, WHIZKID,

she'd typed.

IT'S CALLED *RELATIVITY* AND IT REALLY BENDS YOUR MIND.

MY MIND'S BENT ENOUGH ALREADY. DO I NEED MORE?

DARE YOU!

she had replied, and they had both got sucked into Escher's world. Between them, they bought every puzzle on the market, as the longest, coldest winter in history hit the province.

SO WHICH IS YOUR FAVOURITE?

she'd asked, when they'd completed the last and hardest of the Escher puzzles.

METAMORPHOSIS, FOR SURE. I LIKE THE
CHESSBOARD TURNING INTO A HONEYCOMB AND
THE BEES FLYING OUT AND BECOMING BIRDS.

YEAH, ME TOO. AND THE WAY IT TURNS INTO A
CITY WITH THE WATCHTOWER BEING THE ROOK
ON ANOTHER CHESSBOARD.

I REALLY LIKE THE WAY ESCHER DOES THAT.
THINGS TURNING INTO OTHER THINGS, THE
REAL BECOMING THE IMAGINARY . . .

*   *   *

Joan dipped her spoon in her cereal bowl and sighed.
"I'm fine, Dad. Only bored."

"No more Escher puzzles?"

"We've done them all. They were great. The real
becoming imaginary, and the other way round. I'd
like to visit an Escher world."

Max laughed. "Maybe you can. Or one like it. One of
my program designers is an Escher fan. He says Escher's
ideas have got some intriguing game possibilities."

"He?"

"Jason Bedard. Brilliant kid. Shot through school
and joined MaxCom a year ago. You must remember
him."

Indeed Joan did. She'd met him at the staff party
the Christmas before the accident. None of the guys

had been smartly turned out—it wasn't that kind of party—but Jason had been notably scruffy. He'd claimed her for the first dance, and she hadn't been able to help noticing that the neck of his sweater had been soiled and there was something—was it egg?— on the front. And frankly, he'd smelled as if he hadn't bathed in a week.

"Well, he probably hasn't," Max's secretary Molly had said to her when she'd escaped to the ladies' room to wash her sticky hands. "These young programmers have single-track minds and hygiene just isn't part of their world. Sometimes I have to turn on the fan in my office in self-defence."

As soon as Joan had emerged from the washroom Jason had grabbed her for another dance. She'd tried to talk to him about swimming—but he hadn't been interested. About school—ditto. He'd been into psychology in a creepy way, about the things people instinctively fear—what he called "The Stephen King" syndrome—and had asked her about *her* deepest fears. She'd wondered if he ever brushed his teeth.

It was too bad. That had been her first grown-up dance and she'd persuaded Mom to buy her a new dress for it. But Jason had seemed to be the only unattached male and, unless she'd been willing to spend the rest of the evening in the ladies', she was stuck with him.

"No, thanks," she'd said when he'd tried to grab her for a third dance. "I'd rather sit this one out."

"Oh, come on." He'd pulled her hands and she'd felt herself shrinking away.

"What's the matter? The boss's daughter too good for me?"

"Of course not. It's not that."

"Well, what's the problem? Let's go."

She'd found herself blushing and totally lost her cool. "I'm sorry, but you stink," she'd blurted out, like a four-year-old instead of a fourteen-year-old.

He'd dropped her hands as if she were a snake and turned away. She'd seen the colour flame the back of his neck and his ears, and she'd wished she could have taken the words back, but it had been too late.

*　　*　　*

"You must remember Jason," Max said again.

"Yeah, I guess so," she said, pushing the embarrassing memory out of her head and reaching for her orange juice.

"He's working with Adrienne Harris, my top artist, on a really ambitious project. Something quite new."

"Hmm." Joan wasn't really listening. She had Whizkid on her mind. When she'd asked him what project they should tackle, now that they'd finished the Escher puzzles—more chess or something new—he'd backed out.

BASEBALL SEASON COMING UP. LESS TIME THAN EVER. LET'S PUT IT ON HOLD FOR NOW.

On hold? What about her? Her whole life was on hold.

She'd e-mailed her Australian friend, Anti, looking for sympathy.

WHAT'S HE LIKE?

Anti had asked.

I'VE NEVER SEEN HIM, BUT I IMAGINE HE'S GOT
A LEAN AND INTERESTING FACE, KIND OF LIKE
KEANU REEVES. BUT THIS BASEBALL THING IS
REALLY BORING. SEEMS HE'S GOT NO TIME.

SO? YOU'RE LIVING IN THE SAME CITY. GO AND
CHEER HIM ON.

GOT TO GO,

Joan had typed, and logged off.

Cheer him on, indeed. She imagined herself at a game and Whizkid's face when she told him who she was. *No way. Never!*

It was all very well for Anti to talk, swimming laps in an Aussie pool, getting a tan on Bondi Beach. What did she know about it? Joan pushed her cereal bowl aside and stared out the window. The snow had gone and the ground had dried up. There was a haze of green on the distant aspens.

"I'm so bored," she complained when, later that day, Kathy came to put her through her exercise routine.

"You really should keep up your swimming. It'll bring back your upper body strength as well as take you out of yourself."

"And how'm I going to get into my suit? And get into the pool?"

"I could take you, Joan. And there's a chair lift at the pool. It would be easy."

"It'd be disgusting. Everyone staring. No way. I'd sooner die!"

But Kathy must have talked to Max. He took time off to spend the next afternoon with her. "What's up, Princess?"

"I'm so bored, Dad. And so tired of this stupid chair. And . . ." She stopped herself from saying "and so lonely." That wouldn't be fair to Max, who tried so hard to be a good father to her.

"What about that pal of yours, Whizkid?"

"Oh, I guess he's through with chess and computer games. All he wants to do is play baseball. I wish . . ."

"What, Princess?"

"Oh, I dunno. I wish he and I could have a real adventure together." She sighed. "Stupid, I know, Dad. Forget it." But he didn't.

And that's how it all began.

*　　　*　　　*

When Steve Andersen got back from baseball practice a couple of weeks later and logged on, there was a message waiting for him.

message from Talk.Daemon@maxcom.ca at
18.50

talk; connection requested by
joanna@maxcom.ca

talk; respond with: talk
joanna@maxcom.ca

Steve typed onto his keyboard:

talk joanna@maxcom.ca. HI, JOANNA. LONG
TIME NO HEAR.

AND WHOSE FAULT IS THAT? I'VE GOT
SOMETHING NEW. WHAT DO YOU THINK
ABOUT AN INTERACTIVE VIRTUAL REALITY
ADVENTURE? WAY BETTER THAN ORDINARY
COMPUTER GAMES. IT COMES WITH ALL THE
WORKS—HEAD-MOUNTED VIDEO DISPLAY
WITH 3-D AUDITORY SYSTEM AND FIBRE
OPTIC VIEWING AND FEEDBACK. WIRED
GLOVES WITH SENSORS . . .

HEY, WHAT DOES IT ALL MEAN?

IT MEANS WE'LL FEEL LIKE WE'RE REALLY *THERE*,
AND WE CAN MOVE WHEREVER WE WANT INSIDE
THE GAME WORLD. SO WHAT D'YOU THINK?

VIRTUAL REALITY? I THINK YOU'RE OUT OF MY
LEAGUE, GIRL. NO WAY I CAN AFFORD GEAR
LIKE THAT. OR THAT POWERFUL A PC. MINE'S
STRAINED TO THE LIMIT ALREADY.

THAT'S THE GREAT PART. IT'S ALL EXPERIMENTAL.
WE'RE LIKE GUINEA PIGS TRYING IT OUT FOR THE
COMPANY. ALL YOU HAVE TO DO IS PICK THE
STUFF UP AT MAXCOM INDUSTRIES . . . HEY, ARE
YOU STILL THERE, WHIZKID?

SURE. JUST THINKING. THERE'S GOT TO BE A
CATCH.

BOY, YOU'RE SUSPICIOUS. LIKE I SAID, IT'S
EXPERIMENTAL. WE'LL BE DOING THEM A
FAVOUR.

WHY US?

MY DAD WORKS FOR THE COMPANY. YOU KNOW
THAT. THAT'S HOW WE GOT YOU AN ACCOUNT
WITH MAXCOM. SO HOW ABOUT IT?

OKAY, I GUESS. SURE.

YOU CAN PICK THE STUFF UP TOMORROW. TALK
TO YOU SAME TIME?

YES—SORRY—NO. WORKOUT IN THE GYM AFTER

THE GAME TOMORROW. HOME BY 21.30.

TALK TO YOU THEN. G'NIGHT. :-)

Steve hit Control-C, exited, and switched off his computer. Talking with Joanna was certainly interesting, though she did tend to be bossy. He wondered what she looked like, whether he'd recognize her in a crowd. He imagined her as tall, athletic, with long black hair. In high school, she'd said, and a competitive swimmer. Probably the same age as himself.

But virtual reality? All that high-priced equipment? Would Dad lend him the station wagon to haul it home? And what would he and Mom think of a carload of electronic equipment? A gift from a stranger on the Net? No way! They'd never believe him. They'd think he'd flipped and turned to burglary.

He almost didn't believe it himself. But Joanna had said it was just a *loan*. That was what he'd have to emphasize to Mom and Dad. Especially Dad. To be returned after a test run. Meanwhile, he had other things to worry about.

He took his baseball glove off the shelf and began to oil it, thinking of tomorrow's game. It was important to do well. Important to Dad, who'd just missed being a great player when he was at school, back in the Middle Ages, and dreamed of better success for his son. Only Steve really wasn't that good. Not bad. Just not great.

"Play the last game through in your mind," Coach Rafferty had told them. "Go over your plays. Figure out how they could have been better. Imagine your-self doing every move just right; then play that way in the next game."

Like thinking out moves ahead in chess, Steve thought, rubbing oil into the leather with a piece of soft cloth. He sighed. That's how it was supposed to work. Okay with knights and rooks on a checkered board. He was great at visualizing, no problem. Even out on the baseball diamond, he could see himself clearly, out in right field, with the ball screaming towards him. He visualized his heroic leap, his perfect catch, the throw that would wipe out the other team.

But when it came to an actual game, reality set in, and he'd either fumble the catch or trip or not even be in the right place at the right second. *Let's face it, Steve Andersen*, he told himself. *You'll never be a great player and all Dad's dreams can't change that.*

Maybe he should stick to his studies, as Mom wanted, and forget about baseball. Only, Dad would never forgive him if he didn't at least try for the team. Either way, there wouldn't be much time left over for this new virtual reality game. He hoped Joanna would understand that.

*   *   *

Joan switched off her computer and looked up at her father. "Okay so far." She tried to sound excited for Max's sake. He tried so hard. But this wasn't life.

Just another computer game, not much different from the ones they'd played all winter, except that this one was in virtual reality. _Like 3-D_, she thought. _But still only a game._

"So he'll go for it, this Whizkid of yours?"

"He was a bit suspicious at first. I guess he's not the sort of person who likes getting something for nothing."

"That shows character. I'd have worried about his being your partner if he were a grabber. So how'd you get him to accept the stuff?"

"Told him we were just testing it out."

"True enough, Princess. It's right on the cutting edge, this game. Remember when you talked about Escher's prints?"

"You said Jason and Adrienne were working on a new project."

"Well, the prototype's completed, and they've personalized it especially for you, Princess."

"Personalized?"

"Jason's tailored it to your psychological profile. I gather the game's a zinger."

Joan suddenly shivered, and then told herself not to be paranoid. Jason must have long forgotten that unfortunate incident at the dance the year before. She pulled her attention back to Max, whose face glowed with enthusiasm.

"Keep me up to date on how the game works out, Princess."

"Sure, Dad," she said automatically. Then she

remembered how Mom used to listen to all his schemes. He must miss that. "Sure I will, Dad. And thanks!" She tried to sound as enthusiastic as he was, but it didn't come out that convincingly. He patted her shoulder and turned to stare out the window for a moment. When he turned back his voice was deliberately cheerful. "This partner of yours, Whizkid. What's his real name?"

"Oh, I don't know that. We're anonymous on the Net. That's part of the fun."

"I'm not sure I like the idea of your having a friend I know nothing about. Couldn't you ask him?"

"Uh-uh. I wouldn't want to. If I started asking questions, he'd want to know about me too, wouldn't he? Maybe start talking about us getting together. No way!"

"I could find out who he is without his knowing. When he comes to the factory to pick up his stuff." Max rubbed his chin thoughtfully. "It wouldn't be difficult. I'd feel better."

"Set your spies on him? No, Dad, don't even think of it, please! Promise? It wouldn't be fair. He's Whizkid and I'm Joanna. That's all we need to know about each other."

"And in the game?"

"The same. The team of Joanna and Whizkid against—against what, I wonder?" She tried to sound excited, and this time it seemed to work.

Max laughed. "Don't ask me, Princess. Only Jason and Adrienne know. It's their game. Their rules."

*　　*　　*

The security guard walked briskly along the silent corridors of MaxCom Industries, his rubber soles squeaking against the polished vinyl. He tested each door and paused at the end of the corridor to punch his time clock before turning right. VIRTUAL REALITY LAB. Through the frosted glass he could see the moving glimmer of lights. The two figures hunched over the monitor looked up as he pushed the door open. The kid turned.

"Oh, it's you, Ed. What's the time?"

"Ten o'clock, Mr. Bedard. Will you be through soon?"

"Another half hour maybe." He stretched and turned back to the monitor.

"Good night, Miss Harris. Good night, Mr. Bedard. Don't forget to lock up, will you?"

As the door swung shut, Adrienne Harris continued the argument that the guard had interrupted. "I just don't like what you're doing with this scenario, Jason. It's far too dark. Remember who we're designing it for."

"Not likely to forget, am I?" He laughed harshly. "Miss Toffee-nose Joan Sandow. Miss Boss's Daughter."

"Cut it out, Jason. She's a nice kid, and she's had a really rough time, losing her mother and becoming disabled herself."

"Tough cheese. She's still a spoiled brat."

"What's going on, Jason?" Adrienne looked thoughtfully at her companion. She was twenty-eight and had been in the business since leaving art school. Jason seemed ridiculously young, barely out of the egg. Young. And vulnerable. "You got hurt— that's it, isn't it? She snubbed you?" She saw his face tighten. "Hey, just forget it. These things happen. Don't take it personally."

He shrugged. "That's got nothing to do with it. Anyway, kids like a story to be dark. They enjoy being scared."

"Your story is past scary. It's weird. You're trying to control her mind with those subliminal effects."

"Don't you understand, Adrienne? It's the wave of the future. Not just visual, tactile and auditory effects, but emotional too."

She shook her head. "Not these emotions, not for Joan. I won't go for it. I know you're the designer of this story, but I'm responsible for the graphics, and if you go overboard, I just won't follow you."

"And if I won't change the story line? Will you give up working on the project? The boss won't be pleased. He's set his heart on this little prezzie for his 'princess'."

Adrienne flushed. "I know you're a great designer, Jason, but don't get carried away. If push comes to shove I've worked with Max for nearly six years and you're a newcomer."

"You'd pull rank on me? I don't believe it!"

Adrienne hesitated. *Should* she talk to Max? But a complaint from her would humiliate Jason badly. She shook her head. "No, I'll deal with it my way."

"Like . . . ?"

"I could write myself into the story. I'm not as good a programmer as you are, but I could still do it."

"Like a fairy godmother waving your magic wand?" Jason laughed. "I'm sure you could. But look out! If you interfere in my story, I'll be right there changing it back to the way I want it to be."

She glared at him in the light reflected from the monitor. His overlong hair was tousled and needed a good wash, and he hadn't put on a clean T-shirt all week. All his energy went into designing new worlds. Just a kid needing a mom to clean him up, she'd always thought. But this anger was something else. And how would it spill over into the world of virtual reality? Could he do any *real* damage? Time alone would tell. Somehow, she felt that the moment needed a big gesture, like a salute with swords before a duel. But while she was still thinking of that gesture, Jason unfroze the screen and the story began to roll forward again.

about the author

Monica Hughes, a writer of international acclaim, was born in England and now lives in Edmonton. A popular children's writer on both sides of the Atlantic, she is now the author of 30 books, including *My Name is Paula Popowich!*, *The Golden Aquarians* and, most recently, *Where Have You Been, Billy Boy?* Her numerous literary awards include the Vicky Metcalf Award and two Governor General's Awards. In 1981 and 1982 she received the Canada Council prize for Children's Literature.